# BROKEN PARADISE

## EUGEN BACON

### LUNA NOVELLA #13

D1596061

Luna
Press
PUBLISHING

First published by Luna Press Publishing, Edinburgh, 2023

"Namulongo" short story first pub. in *Chasing Whispers*, Raw Dog Screaming Press, 2022

www.lunapresspublishing.com
ISBN-13: 978-1-913387-32-7

*Mai wani*
*Mawe wange*
My mother.

In memoriam.

# Contents

A GODDESS OF THE WATERS    1

A Sea Ghost Sees This    2
What the Heart Knows    4
A Spell of Displacement    8
A Shriek in Freefall    13
Unassembled    16
The Feebleness of Earth    20
A Coven of Magi    23

NAMULONGO AND THE EDGE OF DARKNESS    27

A Lot of Selfless Running    28
Isolate the Flame from the Wick    33
Put Up the Drone    37
Stay Hungry for the Ocean    40
The Fallout    44
The Ocean Stays Hungry    48
Spell Like It's Survival    52
To See the End, Look at the Beginning    58
First, Ask Me a Riddle    60
Too Much Doom    65
All Things Are Never Equal    69
A Tornado of Flames    72
Shackery-in-a-Cabin    76

Command the Vessel                        80
Even a Fish Makes a Difference            84
A Child, Unlearned                        86
Denouement                                92

THE LUMINESCENT GHOST DRINKS              97

An Urge for Words and Silence             98
The Hurricane Groaned                    101
No Tim Tams, Please                      103
A New Magus Is Born                      106
A Multiplicity, and Death                107
The Awakening                            109
A Darkening Horizon                      110
Together They Are                        113
Hugging the Marula Tree                  120

A GODDESS OF THE WATERS

# A Sea Ghost Sees This

*NAMULEE, NAMULEE… a sea ghost's longing. Hir fog shifts to tell a story of a beginning in the pockets of heaven. Right here in a paradise of one name: Savanna. And this is a tale of four gods and their Goddess Mother.*

*The Savanna was pregnant with locusts and honey. A sweep of golden grasslands awash with eternal light. Whistling thorn trees bore lollipop fruit. Out by the riverine woodlands, you could lick rum straight from the bark of a marula tree—her aromatic fruit eaten fresh, juicy and the size of a plum. There was a baobab that stood 5,000 years old with its fat trunk. It bore pavlova flowers that opened nightly and fell into laden baskets by dawn. In summer the mopane tree, also called the butterfly tree, cast its big shade in the hottest elbow of the low-lying ground. The tree's mopane worms dropped cool and fat—tasty as self-saucing puddings—in self-collecting hampers.*

*The brightness of Goddess Mother drew you in, engulfing you in a swallowing intensity that commanded awe. And her hair! Its cascading blue bounced in a shimmer. She was an all-mother like the universe, and she loved her three handsome but much-flawed sons. Posé, the firstborn, held a gift of sight; he could see anything in the heavens or the Earth, but it didn't mean that he was wise. Tamoi, the second son, was gifted with beauty; you set eyes upon him and were immediately bedazzled. But Tamoi's flaw was conceitedness. Daga, the favourite son, was born gifted with cleverness. His golden touch that brought dead things to life came along with cunning.*

*The sons were not the last of Goddess Mother's woes. She also loved, but was troubled by her only daughter, Samaki, born between Tamoi and Daga. Samaki was a child of the wet season, in her element when rains spoke with thunder. Her eyes shone bright silver when she floated on the universe, casting in baritone the spells she created.*

*A sea ghost sees this.*

# What the Heart Knows

Samaki is floating in space-time. She adores the fusion of dimensions. This is her beloved spot, a place in the universe where she feels singular and infinite. Sometimes when time stops, when she feels connected yet disconnected, she wonders about a four-dimensional manifold, a feeling of paradox, and relativity where she's one yet many.

She casts her eyes into black space and chants her spells.

#

Samaki flies over the Savanna grasslands as a black and white bird dives below her with an ardent cry. She soars above a leopard that is dangling across the branch of a mopane tree, its tail flicking away fireflies. A lioness abandons her fat cub, gives a half-hearted chase of a lone kudu that outsprints her. The cub mewls for its mother, plods with chubby paws towards the lioness, falls on its face.

Samaki floats from levitation and onto the ground. She walks in sandals towards the palace and its state rooms and galleries, garderobes and oratories. She approaches the gatehouse and senses the Goddess Mother, who has a way of appearing quietly. Goddess Mother reminds Samaki of nebulae, dust and gas so bright, impossible not to notice. Especially with that evening fragrance of devil's thorn she's taken to wearing.

Goddess Mother steps into view from nowhere.

"I know when you have a mission," says Samaki. She eyes her mother. "What is it today?"

"I want you to make an effort."

"What have I done?"

"You're late again." Goddess Mother's eyes glitter, diamonds enshrouded in topaz.

They walk into the main hall, where pets that are also guards eye them without moving. There's Rina, the white rhino. Sabi, the sabre-toothed tiger. And Dodo—slow, awkward and dumb. He loves swimming with flamingos in the crystal lake in winter.

Samaki and Goddess Mother cross the great hall with its arched doorway. The hall is lined with marble mantels, hearths and bronze statues of the Goddess Mother in different postures. Here, underneath a clock that's more ornament than anything, is a statue of the all-mother standing. In her arms is a cherub baby who's the golden-haired Daga.

"Tell me again why you're late," says Goddess Mother.

"I was soaked in time," says Samaki. "The spells, you know?"

"No, I don't," says a stern Goddess Mother. "You don't need to practice spelling. You're very efficient with it already."

"I visited Daga in his lab today. He's working on a potion."

"He's always working on potions."

"Will he succeed?"

Goddess Mother laughs. "Who knows with that brain? I

am just afraid that his transformations are profitable only to himself."

Her brothers are gifted, but don't seem to know what to do with their gifts. Daga has wasted his golden touch on the palace, gems in vitreous lustre everywhere. Look at the pillars and walls in agate and quartz. Everywhere blinks in olivine or incandescent hues. The greenish-blue of amazonite in sinks and bathrooms, toilets too! Even faucets gleam sodalite—purple, nosean, lazurite or rich blue—when one reaches to turn a tap. Only gods can tolerate so much shining.

Posé, Tamoi and Daga are already seated. They're smoking cigars in the mauve drawing room with its velvet curtains. Only Tamoi acknowledges her with a nod. 'Sam.'

She nods briskly, ignores right back the other two and goes straight to the bureau. "Port or marula wine?" she asks the Goddess Mother.

"It's always the marula. I can't get enough of it."

Samaki pours the wine into a porcelain flute, offers it to her mother and then pours one for herself. She takes an engraved mahogany chair, shifts it at an angle from the gilded settee next to her brothers. She forces a smile and directs it at Daga.

"Are you making anything fun in the laboratory now?"

"Oh, just a poison that can kill a god. I've been refining it for eons."

She laughs, uneasy. "I didn't think Tamoi annoyed you too."

"Sam!" Tamoi feigns to be wounded, then looks at Posé and Tamoi in a conspiratorial glance the brothers have recently developed. It always unsettles Samaki.

"Sorry I arrived late for our sojourn," she says.

"Time has a way of eluding one when night and day look

the same," says Posé, in his serious, husky voice. "Aurora borealis, aurora australis."

"Are you going scientific on us, again, brother?"

"You're also scientific in your spells. Aren't you a magus—powerful? I've never seen you miss," says Daga.

"Says one of such cleverness, capable of controlling minds," says Samaki.

"Oh, except yours and Goddess Mother's."

"Sometimes you succeed, brother."

"Only when you're weakened."

Samaki feels inside the breast pocket of her ochre-red suit. She pulls out a booklet.

Goddess Mother's eyes flare. "Daughter, put the grimoire away when we're together. You don't need rituals and hexes around your brothers."

Samaki leaves the grimoire alone. What her heart knows is that she's an anomaly in this family. She's been at odds with them since she was a toddler with her spells.

## A Spell of Displacement

Samaki walks alone in the sprawling gardens that stretch out to meet the grasslands. She feels heady from all the marula wine Tamoi kept pouring. She resists the urge to go floating in space-time, looking down and contemplating the humans. Perhaps human families are more together than the families of gods, always fighting to determine dominion over others. Humans don't perceive her as a threat. They don't know Samaki, yet they live around her oceans and seas, her rivers and lakes. Her islands and seabeds. She thinks about sea monsters, how she has command of them all, because she's the goddess of the waters.

Second to the cosmos, the garden offers solace. She personally grew the miracle fruit. She nurtured the baby bananas and their sweet aroma. The papayas and their soft lusciousness. The white star apple and its taste between a lychee's and persimmon's. She loves most the imbe fruit—the acid freshness in its plum flesh.

Samaki also grew the flowers. She adores beauty, just not the Tamoi kind that is full of conceit. She studies her babies. There's the krantz aloe and its orange arrow tips—yellow-green leaves, all juicy and slimy, also edible. The impala lily, sometimes called the desert rose—it is star-shaped and white inside a pink petal. The kudu lily and its wavy margins like a swirling star—its flowers glow white on a succulent shrub, glossy-leafed. She touches the monkey tail, fair inside—wavy green leaves curl like a tail.

#

Samaki is back in her room in the palace. Music drifts up from the drawing room and its gilded piano, one of her brothers playing. They are still together, smoking cigars before they retire to their rooms, all regal with bejewelled chests of drawers and great wardrobes.

Goddess Mother is likely downstairs too, sojourning with her sons.

Samaki feels alone. She takes out the grimoire, studies her new spells. She tests out a chant:

*Kapa moto*
*Tena saba.*

This is the spell of elements: fire, water, air, metal, earth. She experiments with a tiny version of it, unkeen to destroy the palace in a torment of rogue fire. She lights a baby flame on her palm, swirls it. Tosses it up and down above her bed. With this spell, she can command fire. Outdoors, she plays with water, air, metal and earth—commands them too. She moulds and shapes, and the elements listen.

She reads out a new spell:

*Ja bimbi*
*Pa urogi.*

This is the spell of displacement. It imprisons. She doesn't chant it, lest she inadvertently locks herself up, because it must be focused on an object, and right now she's thinking about herself. But she chants the next spell:

*Kuto nipa*
*Pepo hilo.*

This is the spell of embodiment. She morphs into a mermaid, a fishtail for legs, right there on her bed. She laughs at how tickly it feels to wear scales partway down her body. She changes back to herself and chants another spell:

*Muta sita*
*Jangu le.*

This is the spell of growth, and she experiments with her nails. They unfurl into claws, and she draws them back. She alternates the length and shape of her hair. Studies each new look on her tall commode that glints with mirrors, and chuckles. She knows it's the wine. She really shouldn't be doing spells now.

She puts her grimoire on the chiffonier. Picks up a jar and sprays on the nape of her neck its perfume of the flame lily—vanilla and orange blossom. It makes her feel… less lonely. She's wallowing in wealth: the malachite candelabra over there, her jewel cabinet over here, the lavish mattress and its softness of a baby ostrich's feathers.

So why does she feel poor?

#

She sees him, the glint of his beauty, inside her closed eyes. She feels him, how he gropes her negligee. She wakes with a roar.

"Sam…"

"The hell?"

"It's only me."

"The hell!"

She shoves Tamoi from her bed to the floor. He makes as if for the door, then swirls, his attack sudden. His breath is warm against her neck, his smell oozing port and cigar. Strong hands pin her to the bed. Samaki closes her eyes, pays inward attention and chants:

*Ja bimbi*

*Pa urogi.*

The spell of displacement imprisons Tamoi, ropes him in her sheets.

"Sam, let me go!"

She focuses her rage to a point on his forehead:

*Ona jinga*

*Hilo leo.*

It is not the spell of destruction she hasn't yet mastered. Her chant summons *paralymus*, which stops Tamoi from struggling. He's immobile, but breathing. Her spell of elements yanks Tamoi, still roped in bedsheets, and paralysed, from her bed and up on air. His eyes betray his petrification. He wants to scream but can't. She incants again:

*Koma tena*

*Hapa sasa.*

And, with a big cry that's also an explosion, she hurls her hands into empty space.

A gust of wind swirls Tamoi, crashes him through the window, out and away… from the palace like a shooting star.

Goddess Mother is the first to burst into Samaki's room. "What have you done?"

Daga and Posé pour into the room.

"Oh, I saw something fly. Please tell me it's not Tamoi," says Daga.

"You, my brothers, have been plotting against me." Samaki glares at them.

Goddess Mother's eyes burn so brightly. "Have you used a spell on one of your own? Bring him back."

"No." Samaki is trembling in her rage.

"I said—" begins Goddess Mother.

Samaki bellows and a hurricane swirls from her eyes. She's lost in space, the gravity so strong. It's freezing, everything deformed. Now she's a dense ball, antimatter. Her stomach is full of dark galaxies and black holes. Reality, unreality implodes.

# A Shriek in Freefall

"What happened?" Samaki asks weakly from her bed.

The Goddess Mother looks at her kindly. She wipes Samaki's forehead with a wet cloth. "Your tidal force. That's what happened."

"It was a spell of destruction."

"Dear daughter, such a potent spell—against your family?"

Samaki looks away.

Goddess Mother sits on the bed, close to the pillow. She strokes Samaki's head, hums a gemstone and petal song. It's a song of the desert rose and whistling thorn.

Samaki's world lights anew in a shimmer of peridot stars and a wink of carnelian moons.

#

Goddess Mother, Posé and Daga insist, but Samaki will not leave her room.

"Do it yourselves," she says.

"You and I both can fly and reach space-time," her mother gently says. "Your brothers are not as good at it, but they are getting better. None of our powers can break your spell of displacement."

"That tells me you've tried," cries Samaki.

"Every tree has its place," says Goddess Mother. "As do all of you, my children, here in Savanna. Your brother Tamoi too."

"He's what you made him," says Samaki. "No boundaries."

"It's my fault, then, that you've cast him into space. I will teach him boundaries."

"You always defend him, Goddess Mother."

"He is my son!"

"And I am your daughter!"

Goddess Mother's look has a plea. "Does a hen break its own egg?"

"To make room, sometimes, yes," snaps Samaki. "It saves the others."

Goddess Mother takes her hand. "Don't you think your brother is punished enough?"

#

Samaki finds Tamoi at the edge of the heavens where she entrapped him. She lifts the spell of *paralymus*, so he can talk.

"Sam! Thank Goddess Mother you're here."

"You have every reason to thank her," says Samaki. "Why I'm here now."

She lifts the spell of displacement, and the bedsheet sweeps away. Tamoi shrieks in freefall.

*Kapa moto*
*Tena saba.*

Samaki suspends him in space with a spell of elements, and yanks him close with invisible strings.

"I didn't mean anything by it. Sam, I swear!" Tamoi looks

about at the black space upon which he's suspended. "What will you do to me?"

"Not kill you."

Samaki hums her chant:

*Muta sita*

*Jangu le.*

"No!" Tamoi cries as a hideous horn grows where his nose was.

Tamoi touches his horned nose. He looks at the scales on his hands and screams. "Please, Sam. No!"

## Unassembled

*Who would embrace scales and horned nostrils? Not Tamoi. Not his mother or brothers, either. A sea ghost sees this. As Tamoi conspires more with his brothers Posé and Daga—perhaps also with the Goddess Mother—Daga's poison finds its way into a baobab fruit that Samaki bites.*

*She doesn't die, but is bedridden for eons.*

*Soon as she finds her feet, Samaki flees the palace. She arcs from the skies, falls from incandescence, from the city of shimmer, and dives all the way into space-time. A place of darkness that is always night as far as you can throw, far, farther, further still.*

*Alone, restless, she practices on meteors and hones her spells:*

*Njoh wangu*

*Amu kah.*

*The spell of creation generates a companion.*

*A sea ghost is this.*

#

Samaki is weary. She takes one last look at space-time, then back towards the heavens spilling with light. She misses family, flawed as it is.

"Goodbye, my friend," she says to the sea ghost she created. How could sie survive freefall into uncertainty?

*Namulee, Namulee…* the sea ghost's cry. A fog envelops Samaki in an embrace, and finally lets her go.

Samaki's freefall of never-ending blackness is full of melancholy. Exhausted, she floats down to Earth, a place of lonely children. She makes her way through deep rain, falls in mud and hauls herself across unfamiliar ground. She tucks in a cave, finds sleep in what she hopes is a millennium. But she wakes almost immediately.

She takes flight and this time lands at the top of a windswept hill. She doesn't know where she is. What she knows is that she's lonely, miserable in this world. She looks around for anything familiar. Not even the flowers. There are no lucky bean creepers, the kind she'd find in Savanna in winter. She sees a wildflower that is nowhere near the white foxglove, feathered and shaped like a downfacing bell.

She sleeps, lonely as ever, wakes in full light. The cave is a murky abyss.

Dusk again, not eternally lit like Savanna, no pillow-black comfort of space-time. Here she jumps at grass whispers, twig snaps, now opens her eyes to see the stretch of an arrow in a bow, at the same time that she hears *Namulee, Namulee…* a sea ghost's cry.

Samaki leaps from the assassin, hurls a spell of destruction that crumbles him and his arrows—the tips of which can kill a god. Her brothers are close.

A fog enshrouds her—the sea ghost.

"How did you get here?" she asks, but knows the answer of a sea ghost who has followed her from the heavens through the realms, all the way to Earth. Blissful at regaining her companion, Samaki allows a deep sleep in the sea ghost's engulfing fog.

#

Samaki blinks, weary. She forgets then remembers where she is, how she's here. Words are many, her memories deceit. Her world is rot.

Unassembled.

This world has hands and eyes that belong to a monster. She demands to know how long she might be here. The monster shows her a water mirror that says Samaki is the monster. Samaki looks, hopes for clues that tell otherwise. But the mirror on the face of a stream says it again. And again. Samaki is the monster, far, far from home.

#

Samaki and the sea ghost keep moving. They head for the ocean, any ocean.

*Namulee, Namulee…* the sea ghost's cry.

Samaki startles from deep sleep and sees a monster snake slithering towards her. She wrestles with it, ashes it with a spell.

#

*Namulee, Namulee…*

The flying lizard swoops from nowhere. It's wet from a swamp, reeks like sin, and spits lightning. Samaki barks out the spell of battle:

*Jitu gani*

*Hali kili.*
It incinerates the flying lizard.

#

*Namulee, Namulee…*
Samaki leaps from sleep and sees the sea ghost entrapping a firefly vampire in hir mist. The vampire becomes human—killable.

Together, Samaki and the sea ghost take flight.

## The Feebleness of Earth

They reach a city. Its buildings are not as tall as the palace in Savanna, never as big. Yet many people live in them, and there are many balconies and windows. Entryways numbered: *56 / 79 Laneway or 33 Plaza*.

Samaki notices how families are close-knit. She stares wistfully at a passing man, his wife, and a little boy and girl. The children are peddling on bipeds that turn out to be *bicycles* and way different from *motorbikes*, she learns.

She was expecting humans to be splashing about and swimming in rivers and lakes, but there's not much water. There isn't sight of a grassland either—just lots of paths they call *roads*—on which run *cars* that are not houses. She discovers a long snake they call a *train*—stumbles onto it when she flies down onto its *tracks*, nearly decimates it with a spell. She hesitates and the train chugs past to reveal a cargo of humans peering at her with curiosity from the windows.

She finds a botanic garden that's not impressive at one tenth the beauty of her own gardens and their krantz aloes, leopard orchids, impala lilies and water hyacinths back in Savanna.

#

Samaki looks about, glum. This is a world she doesn't understand—it belongs to other gods. Hers are oceans and seas, rivers and lakes, not land. *Namulee, Namulee…* the sea ghost seems unperturbed by it, touching this and that with hir mist. Sie leads Samaki to a strange house that's spilling with people.

"Is this your palace?" Samaki asks a man stepping out of a door.

He laughs. "Where you from, mate?" He points at a sign that says *Waterman*. "Fock me if it's a palace. It's a pub."

The door swings inwards and the pub smells like woodlands gobbled in smoke.

"Give me something to eat," says Samaki to the man at the counter.

"No probs. We got chicken parmas, steak, barramundi, bangers and mash, burgers with the lot," he says. "There's carbonara too. What you want?"

"That nara one."

There's a bird in a cage. It looks like a parrot—that beak, those colours. It's far smaller than the parrots of Savanna. The cage is high up against the wall, near a big box with live humans moving and talking in it. It's a *television*, someone she asks tells her, incredulously, as if her question is a joke.

She looks at baby goldfish endlessly swimming in a tiny tank with mazes, pebbles and mock corals. A couple chase each other into the maze. One fish noses against the glass, peers at Samaki. She imagines herself swimming in the open ocean, catching the water with her strokes, curious goldfish dancing by.

When the *carbonara* comes—"Not nara," the man at the counter says, when he pushes her the plate—it's an awful sticky thing that looks but doesn't taste like stretched mopane worms. The beer is Dodo's piss, not that Samaki has ever tried it, but if she did, it would sip this ghastly. She's pleased to see that they have wine, even one from the marula fruit. Humans step outdoors to smoke bad cigars—they are thinner than the ones her brothers smoke, but they stink just as bad.

She's still contemplating her new surroundings when Posé enters her mind. She sees his grin, and that of Daga. She sees Goddess Mother, worrying and fawning over Tamoi and his horn.

"Brother."

"Sibling."

"You found me," says Samaki.

"Again."

"I thought it was Daga sending the assassins."

"You were mistaken," says Posé in his serious voice.

"I assumed…"

"Because Daga was working on a poison that could kill a god?" He laughs.

"It was you all along controlling his mind. Tamoi's too."

"Goddess Mother has indulged you too long, little Sam."

"Little or not, I'll always be a threat."

"It's a good thing we know right where you are."

"But how? Before, you struggled to read me."

"Your mind is weakened in the feebleness of Earth. Don't you know this, little Sam?"

## A Coven of Magi

Samaki reaches the ocean, stands at its shores with the sea ghost. There's one way to mask her trace—Daga and his assassins will not be expecting it. She's struggled with the idea for a while now, but it's the only way that Posé won't see through it.

She has used the spell of creation once and it gave her a companion. Now she must use it on herself. It's a risky thing to bring life from nonlife. And when it's on yourself…

She touches the water, slips into it.

*Njoh wangu*
*Amu kah.*

She chants, eyes closed, repeatedly.

*Njoh wangu*
*Amu kah.*

The water churns. She has mastered all the spells. Now there's obligation to create.

*NJOH WANGU*
*AMU KAH.*

Samaki cries in agony as she splits in two, then two again to make four. She looks at the quadity of herself. She's Kulwa, she knows this. She's a priestess of oceans and seas. She sees her reflection on the sea ghost's mist—her tight black hair and even face. She doesn't look anything like Samaki. She rolls her eyes and begins to shudder in a chant:

*Mie hapa*
*Langu ziwa.*

It's a unique incantation, her very own. No-one else can use it. Her familiar is the sea ghost. Sie's translucent, male and female, and sie fogs.

"I am Dotto, I know this," says her second self. "I am a priestess of rivers and lakes."

She has satin skin and golden-brown eyes. A smooth face, the shape of an egg. Long, slippery hair. Her sole chant is silent, but they all can hear it:

*Pili mimi*
*Nenda pote.*

Her familiar is swimming at her feet. It's a water demon, a bichwa, with long fingers.

"I am Mazu," says her third self. "I am a priestess of seabeds and islands."

Her eyes are blue-green pearls. She has yellow skin, hair like ferns that fall to her shoulders. She glares and hisses her chant:

*Changu tope*
*Ni zawadi.*

Her familiar noses at her feet. It's a baby whale.

"I am Saba," says her fourth self. "I am a priestess of water creatures." She's bald, gentle. She hums her chant:

*Dudu tari*
*Naita leo.*

Her familiar is a seahorse, right there bobbing on her palm.

The quadity looks at each other, at itself. Together, unbidden, the four magi chant:

*The spell of creation is genesis. The quadity is four. It is always four. Imbalance will bring calamity...*

Kulwa looks at her four selves. She's family, old and family. She's new.

Together they chime all night, sealing the pact of a coven of magi masked in quadity. Parting is never easy, but it's obligation.

Dawn shines bright under a new sun. A whirlwind of sand and water ushers each of the four new magi on their separate path to master that which they command.

NAMULONGO AND THE EDGE OF DARKNESS

# A Lot of Selfless Running

*A SEA GHOST grips Namulongo's hand in a place of lost and found. It wisps in and out in fog, its floating mist swallowing her fears. It ebbs and flows, reacquaints itself with shadow and hiss, sound and image in unevenness that's a questioning, and also a learning. But what's not learning is the fog's growth. Each year's swell is disproportionate to its past. What's not learning is the sea ghost's warmth, how it slips in night and day as Namu tosses and turns in her sleep. What it gives is solace in a familiar face of ambivalent light. At the distant edge of her distraction, the fog dances and smoothes her flaws. It stretches her to a wakefulness that's the best for now, guides her into a chapel that has an altar and a grimoire and then down the basement to a sweeper that's crawling the ocean.*

#

Namulongo's mother knows about her dreams. This is fact, Namu knows. So she doesn't tell her mother everything, especially in the gut of a chore, like now.

"Eee, pampula," exclaims Maé. "What a season you're having, child. I've never seen you guide the sweeper to this big a catch."

"Maybe I was just lucky."

"Luck has nothing to do with it. You've come of age and simply know how to harvest."

"My life feels like a lot of selfless running."

"And that's a selfish thing to say." Maé clicks her tongue.

"I'm just saying—"

"Well, don't."

Namu follows closely, imitates her mother's cleverness with the fish. Maé's hands move swifter with annoyance, her eyes wearing the blackness of a rare pearl, a deep, deeper, deepest ebony. Her eyes gleam silver when she chants before the altar. Maé is a magus of the coven, but she never magics the fish. With Namu by her side, who needs a chant to catch a good harvest from the ocean?

They work tirelessly and isolate the thrashing fish trapped in *Submerse*'s sweepers.

"This one you let go." Maé uses the gentle picker to prong the wolffish and its terrible face down the pressure shoot, and back into the black waters.

"I know, Maé."

"You know because I'm a good teacher."

"Yes, Maé."

At nine cycles, Namu knows a lot about the ocean and its creatures. She knows enough about *Submerse*, her underwater home, and the chores it insists she performs. She bustles from dawn to dusk, bow to stern, running, running in its tight quarters segmented into compartments.

The workshop is one compartment. Here, they make and recycle water, some from the facility that flushes open-valved with a pressured tank. The sleeper is a tiny unit. Here, they take turns in alternating sleep—it's called a warming, where Namu sleeps just off her mother's waking, her warmth on the bed still. It's a shared bunk bed and there's an equally shared locker full of handwoven thermals. The cooker is both a kitchen and a diner. It's next to a hive that has brown bees, all fuzzy-bodied, black-striped. The hive is honeycombed, its honey full of nuts, spice, ocean and smoke.

Near the cooker is a veggie patch. It's more spacious inside than one might expect, and it's reminiscent of something Namu remembers, then forgets. It's as if the growth of each new plant or habitat reinvents the veggie patch, mutates it to optimal conditions. The patch has miniature coconuts that yield sweet and sour water and cream flesh when you crack them. It grows wild lettuce, green tea, chilli pepper, black pepper, baby arrowroot, black nightshade, stinging nettle, shona cabbage, red eggplant, native sunflower, and all. The oxygen chamber has an electrolysis machine that winks green to show the oxygen is right. In the engine room, there's a spare battery and a powered generator that steers *Submerse* through the oceans.

"The moon, the stars—they're our friends," Maé always says.

In the comms room, when the signal is right, Auntie Azikiwe flickers in and out from her enchanted prison. There's a bridge at the top of *Submerse*. The vessel surfaces at dusk, and the watchtower has a periscope for Namu to study the world.

Maé expects much, and Namu gives it. She's good at scrubbing the hulls and the showers and the chambers. She paints to keep *Submerse*'s tough steel from rusting. They don't have a titanium vessel like Aunt Umozi's. The same Umozi who, in her cunning, seized Auntie Azikiwe's submersible and all its power, reinforcing her own physical and charmed supremacy. Aunt Umozi wants Maé and Namu dead. She flickers in and out of the comms transmitter display when she breaches the vessel's firewall, or a surface drone catches a roaming signal. Namu has seen enough of the laughing face and its white, white teeth—let alone her mother's jumpiness when they appear. She's heard enough of the displaced sound to know that Umozi is abysmal, and it started with the Fallout.

Maé will not speak of the Fallout. But Auntie Azikiwe, when the drone picks a signal, and if Maé is absent, has hinted of it. It's a Fallout that happened way before Namulongo, and has cascaded to worse. All Namu knows is that she and Maé are outcast, and Auntie Azi is held captive in her own submerse. All of them are in grave danger. From what Namu has gleaned from stolen conversations, Umozi has grown more powerful since the Embodiment, but no-one will explain the details.

"Can't you get back in favour?" Namu once asked Maé.

"That's beyond question."

Today, Namu looks at the sweeper's harvest. She isolates the fish in buckets. She remembers everything Maé taught her, because Namulongo is a curious one. And curiosity is good for learning. She isolates fish by shape and hue. The silver and blue of the baby bluefin. The treble fin of the mud-coloured cod. The untidy splotch of the flounder. The sleek line of the silver bass. The leopard spots of the trout. Today is a very good catch.

Some play dead fish. *Stun those first.* That's what Maé likes to say. *Hold them by the tail, give a solid whack on the head. Or, if you know where the brain is, pierce it with a blade tip.* Namu knows where the brain is. Sometimes an auto-stunner does the job. *Put the head in first.* It's humane that way. Because playing dead means being cunning. And that kind of sly means the fish's woe is more. They know if you pour an ice slurry over them, and play deader, until they can't. It's cruel to suffocate fish. To see them gasp for air and convulse. To see them contort their bodies until the thrashing goes weak. *Behead quickly, gut,* says Maé. Or just gut. Vertical along the base, peel the tail back. Pull the guts, bone the fillet. Now the fish is really dead. And fresh. Leave the carcass in the cool reefer, until it dumps the smell of the ocean.

"Go and have a splash," says Maé.

"But I washed this morning."

"Eee, pampula. I've never known a girl to hate water. We have lessons soon after, no?"

"Yes, but—"

"But nothing. You purify to cast a spell. And, after the lesson, dinner."

Maé doesn't get that it's not the water that Namu dislikes. It's the restraint that comes with it. Drip, drip, recycle, drip. From an early age, Namu has understood that what she needs is tiny wetness, turn off the faucet. Soap, drip, drip. Dry. Even brushing her teeth is on drip, drip. Wet the brush, turn the water off. Brush to and fro, *remember the tongue.* To and fro, don't forget the cheeks. Spit, turn the water back on. Drip, drip.

Namu is a water creature. It's torment to withhold water for one whose spirit is water. So she avoids the washing in the manner her mother demands, same as she dislikes sleeping. The bunk is a coffin. Her awareness of the tomb that is her home is big, because that very home also drifts through the ocean and its endless flow.

## Isolate the Flame from the Wick

Namulongo and her mother kneel by the altar inside a candle-lit chapel on the lower level of *Submerse*, just above the basement.

"I'll teach you to light the flame different," says Maé.

"Why?"

"Your borrowed spell is lacking. Soon you must whisper your own chant, not mine."

"But I don't have an incantation."

"You'll find it."

"How?"

"Sometimes people dream an 'own' chant. Sometimes you create one."

"I don't need magic language. Maé, I don't want to become a magus."

"You're born to the coven."

"Am I, Maé?"

"Eee, pampula. This sacred place is not for arguing. Fetch me the grimoire."

Namu lifts the magic tablet from its lectern, left to the altar. She hands it to Maé, seated cross-legged on a carpet of cured antelope skin.

"What did I teach you about this text?"

"It's a book of shadows. It has your thoughts, recipes, spells, rituals and hexes—every single one of them personal to you."

"Soon we'll start on your grimoire. Now do as I do."

Maé rolls her eyes and begins to shudder in a chant:

*Inasa bwira*

*Nada ina.*

Flames go out in the array of candles. "Light them again."

Namulongo casts her hand, palms out as if to summon, or to channel. She gazes inwards, sways in a chant:

*In asa bwi ra*

*Na da ina.*

The flame on the wicks flickers weakly.

"Walk me through it," says Maé. "What are you trying to do when you spell?"

"What you asked. I want to make the spell talk."

"Eee, pampula. That's what is going wrong. You need to *talk the spell*. You must *become* the spell—don't think yourself through it."

"I don't understand, Maé. I never will."

"A spell is about belief. Feel it here." Maé touches Namu's head. "And here." Namu's chest. "And here." Namu's stomach. "Now straighten up and do it right."

*In asa bwi ra*

*Na da ina*

"Better. See how the flame is bold? This time I want you to toss it."

"How?"

"Isolate the flame from the wick."

*In asa bwi ra*

*Na da ina*

"Say it like you own it. Draw deep, then breathe your intent in a quick release."

*In asa bwi ra—*

"Child, there's not enough on your breath. Your throat isn't even moving. You need to hang onto belief until the spell homes."

"I'm trying, Maé!"

"Try harder. On a battlefield, if you leave a spell hanging, enemies will pounce. They read you like their own grimoire."

*In asa bwi ra—*

"Where's your conviction?"

"I'm doing my best. How can I succeed if you keep intruding?"

"Because it kills me to see you doing it wrong. You have the right 'initiate'. What you need is a good 'finish'."

*In asa bwi ra!*

*Na da ina!*

Namu heaves forward and throws her arms. Orange-blue flames surge from the wicks. They shoot to the chapel's tough steel roof and flutter in a sizzle, dead on their fall.

"Child." Maé lays a hand on Namulongo's shoulder. "The spell has too much carry. You lost your temper."

"Then stop pushing me!"

"Know composure, even in distress. Never let the enemy read your weakness."

"It's hard to find the craft when you don't want it."

"Feel the spell."

"I need time to settle, Maé."

"Composure is all the settle you need."

By the end of the lesson—Maé still pushing her relentlessly into the world of spells—Namu is spent, body and mind.

"The best time to find your core in a spell is when you need it the most," Maé is saying. "Endure the challenge—an attack can happen quickly. Sometimes all you need is to keep the enemy at bay until help arrives." She ruffles Namu's plaits. "That's the last lesson for today. Accept when you need help. Now, go take a nap."

"You said dinner after. I'm not little anymore—I don't need naps!"

"Even while I surface *Submerse*, then you'll wake for a swim? Trust Bibi, she'll guide you."

The fog of Maé's familiar—the sea ghost—envelops Namu. She finds herself in the bunk bed, her mother's voice a whisper in the distance.

#

*A nap is not a game of statues, just a holding of breath. Sleep, child, in the season of the oceans. Today is upwelling. Seabirds nest and, when you rouse, you can watch whales leaping in the rise and fall of spring winds. I'll make you a flower pickle that protects you from the edge of darkness. Hibiscus petals, sunflower oil, vinegar, thyme and garlic, all sealed in a jar with a spell of origin and conquest. One lick will sigh out the blackness after sundown. Next lick, it'll march you to the horizon, out to see a victory. The battle belongs to you, child. Bloom, bloom, this moonlight, sleep in the ocean's belly.*

*Maga kasi… Osi osi.*

*A sea ghost hums this.*

## Put Up the Drone

Namulongo wakes to a sensation of floating. She remembers drifting to a faraway place.

Then someone calling: "Namulongo." Her head is light.

"Namu! Put up the drone. It's your auntie."

"Maé—"

"The signal is bad. Do it now."

Namu climbs down the bunk, finds her knees and races inside tight walls to the comms room next to the engine room. She dials the special transmitter. The signal on the sound waves and the microphone look good. She boosts the audio amplifier and presses the button that commands the visual drone out of the tower, now on the ocean surface, as *Submerse* goes to rise at the turn of dusk.

Namu joins Maé in a protected control chamber, secured as extra defense from Umozi. She puts on her goggles. There's Auntie Azikiwe, chest up on the screen, bobbing in what looks like space, but it's a compartment inside her submersible where she's imprisoned. The blue-green pearls in her eyes light with recognition. Her hair resembles ferns, the slippery kind that falls to her shoulders. She's yellow-skinned, sinewy-framed.

"Chile, you've come of age, your mother tells me." Her

sweet voice in song.

"It's lonely here."

"But you have me, no?" says Maé. "You have no need to worry your aunt with the little things."

"… your own familiar—" Auntie Azikiwe's sound is breaking in and out.

Namu is not strong on magic, but she likes very much the idea of having her own familiar, like Maé and Auntie Azi.

Auntie Azikiwe's familiar is Walli, a whale. She clicks, whistles, pulses and blows air from her nose. A whale that calls—Namu would love that. Or a brook horse that lets her ride its back in foggy weather. Or a water sprite, gap-toothed and woolly-haired, moving between worlds of the living and the dead. No, a dolphin or a whale are enough. But… Namu feels sad. Auntie lost Walli to Umozi. Miniatured into a house pet, a most cruel thing.

"… remind me of myself, so bright—"

Namu agrees that she's bright, and likes it that Auntie Azikiwe sees herself in Namu.

Maé peers at the screen. "Azi, are you well?"

"… don't know my coordinates—"

"We'll find you, my sister."

"… at the edge of darkness—"

"Give us a better clue, Azi. Are you imprisoned in your own submersible still?"

"… can't control it… displacing me with spells… scatters my signal every few—"

"Just hang on tight."

"… don't have long… By the time we're done on this call—"

"Stay sane, dear one."

"… elsewhere—"

"Be careful. Umozi is getting more dangerous daily."

"… give anything to see the world, to see you—"

"You cannot cure spite, but we'll beat Umozi at her game."

"… running out of food, air and water—"

"Keep using what magic you have left." Maé's gaze at Namulongo is full of message. "Namu needs to learn more magic. But we'll reach you."

"We'll find you, Auntie Azikiwe."

"… mother tells me you have an appetite for spells—"

"I want to be a land voyager," says Namu.

"Eee, pampula. You're a child of the water. Why do you wish to abandon it?" reproaches Maé.

"… isten to your moth—" A sound scratch, then a screech. Auntie Azikiwe glares, wobbles in broken signal and Namu hears the remnants of a chant:

… *ozi tasi*—

The screen goes black.

"Azi? Azi!"

"Auntie Azikiwe!"

"Child, you see why I need you to focus on the spells?"

"We'll find her, Maé."

"We must. None of that nonsense about land voyaging."

# Stay Hungry for the Ocean

Namu stands on the bridge, faces outwards at the yawn of the horizon. She's surprised it's still light, though it's actually dusk. *Submerse* is pre-set to rise to the surface at sundown. In the belly of the metal tube of her undersea home, it's impossible to keep time. Looking out at the waters, Namu feels at one with the ocean.

Dark waves nuzzle each other in a playful stretch, now apart, now they belong together. That which binds them is old and new, just like Namu. She looks out to where she yearns to swim across, and wonders where she might go if she leapt. But she's uncomfortable with the thought, unsure if she crossed the light to the edge of darkness… would she ever want to come back?

She understands the seasons of the oceans. In Upswelling, creatures of the water nest, and she can watch the whales. Winterstorm brings turbulence. A winter squall shimmers frosty air on the cool waters, so rough. In Oceanic, the tide is relaxed, at its quietest. The surface gets warm, the water clear.

A silhouette of birds soars above the ocean.

Namu strips naked from her thermal tights that are ultralight and conserve heat. Her sets are woven in bright colours of summer, rainbow, peach, apple, cherry, blood orange, sunflower, but mostly fruit colours. Unlike her mother's bland colours: grey, navy or black ones. Namu changes sets sparingly, to save the washing. She folds today's papaya-hued ones over a swivel chair inside the tower, pitches forward and torpedoes. She loves the feel of the black water on her skin. It's water that goes and goes across all reaches. She catches it in her palms, releases and lets it flow between her fingers. She streamlines on a float, then flutter kicks, kick… her body swivelling away, away… from *Submerse*.

She listens to the short calls of a storm-petrel. It whines like a seal pup.

*Namulee, Namulee…* she hears the sea ghost's gentle call.

Bibi is translucent, both male and female. Sie can melt in the sun, puddles into water. Sie's a fog when it's cooler. Namulongo turns, reluctant. She faces the vessel that is her home. Is it also her prison? No, it's nothing like Auntie Azikiwe's fate. She pitches upwards, a dolphin on water, explosive from the hips through the feet. She splashes again and again, then sculls vertical, treading water.

*Namulee, Namulee…*

Sometimes when the water is clearer, a pale blue, the light of luminescent creatures matches the moon's. Tonight, she feels the brush of something past her toes, that's all. She can't see below the surface, but knows how deep the waters go.

*Namulee, Namulee…*

Namulongo floats on her back in a one-arm swim. She feels the gentle swell of waves on the flat waters.

Bibi's fog warms Namu as she pulls on the handwoven thermals, and steps back inside the hatch to lost time. She finds Maé in the cooker. She's adding shrimp in a layer on a pan, removing them as they turn pink, start to curl. She drizzles sunflower oil, salt, pepper. Pulls from the baker a pregnant loaf.

"It smells like I'll be eating 'delicious'," says Namu.

"No thanks to me," says Maé. "You and the sweeper, and the flour."

"I didn't do much."

"You roasted the sunflower seeds just right, ground them like someone's paying. Child, why don't you sit? Have a little cassava wine." Maé passes the calabash, breaks the bread. "To the richness of the ocean."

"And the strength of belief," responds Namulongo.

They eat in silence. Namu wonders at the shimmer in the black pearls of Maé's eyes. "The water was calm?"

"You know it was calm, Maé. I don't know if it's me or you, or Bibi. The water is always calm."

Maé's studious gaze, then: "Your hunger for it… Child, you'll always stay hungry for the ocean."

"I want to voyage the land."

"If the gods wanted us to be land folk, we'd have been land folk."

"Sometimes we make our own fate, Maé."

"Action, not words, no?"

"In magic, words have power—you said so, Maé. No?"

"You know it's unessential to speak. Silence, especially now, can be bliss."

#

*Dinner is no civil war, but missiles keep coming across their fundamental differences. At the point of death, if it's the point of death, all they'll remember is wine—not the vinegar kind. They'll pick their way across seasons that hum tender and sing fresh. They'll step into reach and find truth. They'll forget the semantics of filial war. Rebirth is reconstituting oneself. It's slipping from a speckled sun and treading in semitone above the minor 5th to a blush moon. Rebirth is whistling bridges that gather reflections and walk their true selves between petty distinctions and cross-lined gaps.*

*A sea ghost ponders this.*

## The Fallout

A scratch on the comms room, then a crackle.

Crackle, crackle. "Namulongo. Namu!"

Namu and her mother leap in a stampede. They fall into the soundproofed control chamber. The audio is crisp. Auntie Azikiwe bobs in space sharper than they've seen her. The jungle in her fern hair is wild. The pearls in her eyes are a richer colour of the ocean vacillating between blue and green.

She speaks urgently to Maé. "It's cycles now. Namu is grown, maybe—" song of wind and dawn in her voice.

"She's still a child, Azi."

"I'm not as powerful as before. Fighting Umozi's spells has weakened me. Keeping alive is weakening."

"We're doing our best, Azi."

"I feel trapped in a winter storm, yet I'm inside somewhere."

"You must be far, because here it's a quiet night."

Namu hears a terrible scream, as if someone is strangling a dragon.

"Azi!"

"Auntie Azikiwe!"

Her eyes are panicked. "I must go! Umozi is using me as bait to find you!"

"Take care!"

"… cast a homing spell—" a wavering sound yet delicate as a reed in her voice.

"Don't do anything that will enrage her even more."

"… too late—"

The screen zooms onto Auntie Azikiwe's swollen belly.

"Eee, pampula, Azi! What have you done? Why?"

"… life is miserable as it is… worst that could happen?"

"Umozi, that's what! She's the worst that could happen."

"… necessary—"

"You should only use the spell of creation at your hour of death. To keep the quadity. That's how it's always been. The spell of creation is forbidden!"

"… never stopped you—"

Maé turns her head towards Namulongo, who suddenly comprehends.

"Eee, pampula. See what you've done."

"—about time she knew… my back hurts… hungry all the time, crave soft stone—"

Namu hears a scratch, then a screech.

"Azi!"

"She's coming!"

"—if she knows… communicating… she'll move me another place—"

"Auntie Azikiwe!"

The vision goes black.

Maé removes her goggles at the same time as Namu lifts hers.

They look at each other a long time. There's sadness in Maé's gaze, and Namu feels rage in hers. She's breathing hard.

"Your auntie loves you. She didn't mean to upset you."

"She?"

"Child—"

Namu leaps back, as if Maé's touch might burn. "Am I the Fallout?"

"I can expl—"

"I don't want to hear it from you." Namu can't break the tremor in her voice. "I never want to hear it from you!"

\#

*An unborn child folds into the powers of the moon and patterns into raindrops. She's formed by belief. Her palm clasps life in an art of fiction, charts and fortune.*

*A mother wraps a shawl over her belly, plants a fingertip kiss on her bub.*

*A sea ghost sees this.*

\#

Namu distracts herself with chores as her mother sleeps. She climbs to the tower, steps out of the hatch. A cormorant grunts as it takes off from the metal surface. Oink, oink! It circles the air and grunts as it lands back on *Submerse*. Oink, oink! It stalks, and is large this near, a glossy black, sheeny white. It cocks its head, glares at Namu with its green eye circled orange in a patch on its face, then loses interest. It wobbles its bare throat, opens its grey hooked bill and regurgitates fish.

Namu cuts loose the drone in an action that will offset Aunt Umozi's tracker.

*In asa bwi ra!*

*Na da ina!*

The drone erupts in flames on the water, burns itself out, as the cormorant grunts its disdain in flight.

Inside the hatch, Namu wipes down and adjusts the periscope in the looking tower. She closes the hatch, steps back into the windowless *Submerse*. In the engine room, she checks buoyancy, resets the radar and listens for echoes off the seabed.

Once, she caught the signal of a human submarine ten days away. She steered from it, rewrote the satellite feeds on her itinerant world disconnected from humanity.

Gently, she sinks the vessel, glides in the direction of the next guess at a rescue mission.

# The Ocean Stays Hungry

They avoid each other. But inside such close quarters bumping is inevitable when practising rotating sleep. Namu prefers hiding near the pressure hull—the metal that keeps water out. The layout is just so, there's almost a cubicle they sometimes use as storage. The inner hull is resistant to pressure, the outer hull waterproofed.

But Namu can't hide forever in her thoughts. Chores, she needs chores. The shower and its recycled water, drip, drip, three blinks, drip, drip, is in unblemished condition. In the engine room everything is running fine: fins, diving planes, hydroplanes, propellers that push it forwards, the swivelling flaps for tilt, climb, sink or float.

Her smile is wry. She's been too efficient in her chores. There's not much with which to distract herself in her little city under water. Still, she checks the oxygen chamber—it's lit green and the electrolysis machine is farming good air for *Submerse*. She scrubs inexistent grease and amine from the floors and walls. She visually inspects the hull and mixes plant dye. She scrapes peels onto a drop cloth and uses a putty knife to even the surface. She spreads paint with a roller to prevent rust. She checks the compact machine, ejects trash from the watertight exit in the hull.

#

She can't help it, but water is calming. She's up on the tower, level with water. She puts her fingers in the warm black water and wants to weep. If she looks too closely her life is neither a bell nor a shell. Nor is it a song. It's been like this since the metaphor of her birth. One step, two steps, she knows a spell, not a prayer. She knows how to get naked. She bends down and forward from the hips, slips rather than throws herself into the ocean.

She tilts herself to float on her back, her head close to flat on the water. She pushes back with her arm, completes a stroke. Kick, kick, flutter kick, as painful thoughts of her parentage roost home. Maé made her using a spell of creation.

Today, it's too deep for snorkelling. When she can, she finds little treasures she likes to think are gifts Auntie Azi has placed for her to find on the seabed: pearls, shells, sea amulets, coral gems... Namu is a collector, both with her hands and eyes. She stores in her memory what she sees. The muddy sheen of the halibut as it glides by. The fluorescent peach of the rock fish. The silver and yellow of the yellowtail, hence its name; it dances away when she makes as if to catch it by its wide tail. The ugly yawn of the grey lingcod.

She wonders if her familiar, when she gets one, might be a wary one—like the pygmy seahorse. It might be a radiant one—like the cherubfish and the tropical blue on its sunflower nose. It could be a shy one. She'll nudge it out from shyness with her fingers if it were a yellowhead jawfish burrowed in sand, shells or rock. She wouldn't mind a pipehorse—shaped between a seahorse and a pipefish. She's not sure about a tiny eel—worming, burrowing in soft sand, swaying in currents.

Never the frogfish—all the bumps on its skin, but she might learn to love it. She doesn't really have to love a familiar, just to respect it in a symbiotic partnership. At most, she'll feed it plankton.

As she kicks back to the tower, something playful swims in and out of her vision. At first she thinks it's a baby dolphin. She doesn't mind a dolphin for a familiar—she'll call it Dolpho. She'll watch how it moves fast in the water, blowing bubbles and all chatty. This one is chatty. It's white and black. It nudges her stomach from below, as if pushing her to the surface. It whistles, clicks, squawks. She wonders what it's saying.

She climbs out of the water. It moans, barks, groans and yelps. Looking down from the tower she realises it's not white and black, and certainly not a dolphin. She could have sworn it was the biggest tilapia she has ever seen, but fish don't whistle or click, bark or groan, get all playful in the water. How can her familiar be a tilapia? What would she even call it! Pia? Tipa? Seeing how it nudged her with its bottlenose to the surface, maybe the fish might help her if she were sick or injured. And she'll certainly know the plankton or small fish—headfirst—to feed it. With those rows of baby teeth, it's a wonder it didn't bite her.

It's anyone's guess, but Maé says it's time Namulongo got her own familiar.

A blackheaded gull screams out yonder. Namu wonders if perhaps she's got it wrong, and her familiar is a bird. She watches as the fish swims away, farther, farther into the endless blackness of humping waves.

The water is unfinished.

A shadowy moon on the horizon casts a silhouette on the glistening ocean. It begins to rain. Fat drops from the sky fall down, down, and the giant water gobbles each wet pearl, only to reform around itself. No matter what or how much falls into it, *drip, splashity* or *splash!* the ocean stays hungry. Like Namulongo. Restless and open to the sky.

Unfinished.

## Spell Like It's Survival

"Look at this," says Maé.

Namulongo takes the brand-new book and its cover of tempered bark from her mother. She opens it and gasps. "It's unwritten."

"It's yours."

"My grimoire?"

"Your very own. And this." It's a quill pen. "But you must make your own ink."

"How?"

"I'll show you. If you can make plant dye, then you can make ink. You can write in whatever colour you want to write your instructions and divinations. A grimoire doesn't grow in a day."

Maé's eyes gleam silver:

*Inasa bwira*
*Nada ina.*

"There. No-one can write in it, only you. And look here." Maé runs her fingers along a second lectern, also brand new, next to her own on the altar. "It's a placement for your grimoire."

"I'm good with my hands. I could have carved it myself."

"Eee, pampula. This sacred place is not for ungratefulness."

Namu bows her head. "I'm sorry, it's just a little—"

"Overwhelming?"

"Yes."

"Come and sit with me."

They are cross-legged on the carpet of antelope skin. Maé lifts a tiny calabash. She swirls a red liquid that smells like the innards of a rotting wolffish. She dips two fingers and lines the corner of Namu's eyes to her cheekbones.

"I don't like how it smells."

"I'm not asking you to eat it."

"Maé! Will you ask me to?"

"No. It's a ritual bath—today's lesson is a special one. Light the candles."

Namu gazes inwards, sways in a chant:

*In asa bwi ra*

*Na da ina.*

"Mhhh."

"Did I not incant well?"

"You can do better."

"But the flame is bold. Look. Do you want me to isolate it from the wick?"

"I did not ask you to do more than light the candles."

"I'm no good. I'll never be as good as you."

"You'll be, when it's right. Your spell memory is good. You just need better instinct."

"All I can be is a spare."

"Even a fish makes a difference. This sacred place is not for self-pity." Maé's gaze is sharp. "Are those tears? Stop this rubbish."

Namu wipes her checks with the back of her hand.

Maé touches her lightly on the shoulder. "What you bring to the altar is crucial. Cultivate the eyes of your magic."

"I don't know what you mean…"

"Remember what I said. A spell is about belief. Feel it here," on Namu's head, "and here," Namu's chest, "and here," Namu's stomach. "Today we're doing the spell of battle. When an attack happens, there's no time for self-pity. Do you hear me?"

Namu nods, a lump in her throat still.

"Good. To tell you the truth, I think you're gifted with fire. You're a child of water, but you might surprise us with something more. It might be that your familiar will be a dragon."

"A water dragon?"

"A fire one." She studies Namulongo for a while in silence, then says: "Now. I want us to go over the main things you've learnt about spells."

Namu clears her throat. 'There are—"

"Louder."

"There are seven main spells. The spell of elements—with it, you command fire, water, air, metal and earth."

"Good."

"The spell of displacement—this one summons imprisonment, like what Aunt Umozi has done to Auntie Azi."

"An unfortunate thing that we are working to make right."

"The spell of embodiment—it allows you to become the other. This spell can also be a spell of heralding, or a homing. A powerful magus can use it to send help or an assassin."

"I'll practice embodiment with you today, after you tell me the remaining spells."

"The spell of growth works on life that already exists. You

use it to manipulate plants, hair, nails, small animals and the like. The spell of battle helps you disperse, deter, injure, paralyse, misdirect or intercept the foe. You can summon paralymus to temporarily inhibit a foe so they can't move closer or do you harm."

"Child, you are a sponge. Your theory is astounding. We just need you to get practical."

"The spell of destruction allows you to destroy, burn and disintegrate."

"You must never ever summon this spell unless your life depends on it."

"The spell of creation is forbidden. You use it when you've mastered all the other spells and there's obligation to bring life from nonlife."

Maé avoids Namu's gaze. "Good," she says, too sprightly. And then, all serious: "What do you know about a bichwa?"

"It's a water demon with long fingers that drag you deep into the water."

In a blink Maé wisps into nothing, then billows. A multiplicity of eyes gleams from the dark mist. A beast leaps out of the haze and backhands Namu across the face. The ferocity of the swipe strikes Namu headfirst against the far wall. She begins an incantation as the beast charges towards her through the chapel. It knocks down Namu's spell with a counter and lunges, claws drawn. Namu gazes inwards, throws her palms forward in a chant:

*In asa bwi ra!*
*Na da ina!*

The bichwa falls mid-flight to the ground and shapeshifts back to Maé.

"That was a good intercept," she says.

"What was *that*?"

"To see is to know."

"I don't need you to embody a bichwa!"

"You show good commitment. I like it that you now understand the spell of embodiment."

"How is that a lesson?"

"When an attack happens, you won't always have time or space to respond. Sometimes you're lucky if you get a look, that's all."

"I could have decimated you, Maé!"

"You need extra reach for that. Child, you haven't mastered it."

"Is that blood from your eye?"

"It's nothing. You look like you're in trouble—you haven't moved."

"Aawww."

"Is it your ribs that you're clutching?" Maé offers a hand. "Here, let me—"

"Aawww."

"It's just a bruise, nothing serious. But you'll be sore."

"Aawww."

"Take a few minutes. You need a breather."

"What I need is my mother to stop attacking me."

"It's just a bichwa."

"A big one."

"That's a baby one."

"It's still big."

"It matters not."

"To me it does. The opponent is too much."

"Doesn't look it. Only a fool expects a similar-sized opponent. Clean up the mess and find me in the cooker." Maé turns at the doorway. "Just so you know, that spell was just flicking a finger. In a real battle, all you do with a flick like that is agitate them."

"I did nothing wrong!"

"It's a scrapping start, but you'll get it. Spell like it's survival. Our lives could depend on it."

Namu feels undone. She's at a loss about whether to bellow or curse.

Maé, still at the door, is unfinished. "I can smell you from here. I've never known a girl to dislike water. You're too salty. At least take off those thermals."

## To See the End, Look at the Beginning

Namulongo tends the veggie patch to compose herself before preparing a meal. The sunflowers are doing well. They yield strong-flavoured seeds that make good oil. She uses a cold press to remove the hulls, breaks the seeds into smaller pieces and runs them through the warm press of a steel roller to squeeze out the oil. She enjoys the aroma of roasting seeds in a pan, stirring them frequently. She then grinds them into a fine meal texture and lets the blend cool. She pours it through a strainer, and sieves out the oil.

Maé has also taught her to make plain flour. Namu's thinking this as she digs out an arrowroot for dinner, snaps some black nightshade leaves and shoots. She plucks some nettle. Sometimes she wonders if Maé likes her at all. Namu is not sure what's the distinction between tough love and soundless hate. But Maé's love or hate is filled with sound. She wraps her barbs with adages:

"To see the end, look at the beginning."

"Be lost to know the way."

Now she sits unperturbed, full-lipped, with her tight black hair and smooth sheen on her skin, as if nothing happened. She's knitting new thermals with special needles. The rich melon hue suggests the thermals are for Namulongo.

Namu is good at cooking with limited produce. She peels, washes and steams the arrowroot. She blanches the nightshade and stir-fries the stinging nettle to add taste. It goes best with turnips but also works with arrowroot. Sometimes she uses it in a soup, and Maé can make nettle beer.

Namu fillets a fish vertical along the base, peels the tail back and bones it. She adds it to the steamer, takes it out before Maé can say, "You're overcooking it."

Maé prefers live crab or lobster, boiled alive. Looks and tastes better that way. The shock of a scalding makes the legs fall off. Kills bacteria too, no food poisoning. All she needs is a pan of salted water, heated not too long. The crab or lobster is already dead in a few blinks. Leave to cool. There are no consequences for dinner.

"To the richness of the ocean," says Maé.

"And the strength of belief," responds Namu.

For how long? Namu imagines herself on land, all the wind racing in laughter behind her as they run.

She wants to voice this to her mother, but instead says, "Do you want extra pickle?"

"The octopus one."

"Okay."

## First, Ask Me a Riddle

Up on the tower, the air shimmers. There's no sight of land all around, just waves and waves of the ocean.

*Sheesheeshaashaa.*

At first, Namu is not sure she's heard it right. But the whispers rise again from the water.

*Sheesheeshaashaa.*

And then she hears a distressed cry, *Namulee, Namulee…* the sea ghost.

Bibi in hir fog is immobile at the hatch, unable to seep out. Namulongo knows without asking about the paralymus spell. It's a spell of battle. She looks around for Aunt Umozi, or her assassin.

*Sheesheeshaashaa.*

It's then that Namu sees the nymph. It slips from the water's churn. The creature is a knot of guts and twine that roams in shape until it morphs into a blue-skinned beast of many heads and tails. Its nose is flat, its mouth lipped. Its cheeks are as plump as a newborn's. It arrows a missile of crabs and starfish in the colours of blood. The gore inks with the nymph's vomit in a rainbow. The ocean humps and the black skies swirl in a tall tale, legend or dream that's just too real for Namu.

Maé warned her she might encounter a nymph in an underwater cave. She told her how one may appear as a fluorescent male. How it can conjure storms and wear many faces that lure the young into the water.

*Sheesheeshaashaa.*

"See something you like?"

*You, you, dear child, child…*

"Mustn't you first ask me a riddle?"

The blue nymph rises on tentacles above water. *What is light as fog, fog, but you cannot hold it for long, long?*

"If I solve your riddle, will you leave me alone?"

*Of course, course…*

"Have I reassurance to trust your word?"

The nymph laughs. *No, no…*

Namulongo thinks of Bibi, the sea ghost, but has anyone tried to hold sie for long?

*What is light as fog, fog—*

"I think it's a spell," says Namu.

*Wrong, wrong. Try again, again…*

"How about one's breath?"

*True, but it won't count, count…*

"You said I could trust you!"

*If you solved, solved, in one go, go…*

"Then ask me another riddle."

*What's in a cave, cave and has one hundred eyes, eyes yet cannot see?*

"But I am of the ocean. How would I know what lies in a cave?"

*What, what…*

"I think it's a honeycomb?"

*What house is dark, dark, it has not lights, lights…?*

"But I already answered your riddle."

*Time waste, waste… what, what… is dark, dark…*

"The ocean's belly."

*Wrong, wrong. Try again, again…*

"A tomb."

*True, but it won't count, count… Sheesheeshaashaa… so hungry…*

Namu gazes inwards, locks her fist, and wills a spell.

*In asa bwi ra!*

*Na da ina!*

*I command you to leave me!*

The blue nymph laughs.

*Maybe, maybe, try again, again…*

Namu summons her belief.

*In asa bwi ra!*

*Na da ina!*

*I said leave me!*

The blue nymph laughs as its tentacles climb from the water and onto the tower.

*Fail a simple, task, task, to finish a riddle, riddle… Now a spell, spell? Your blood so tasty, tasty… pull you under…*

*Namulee, Namulee…* Bibi's distressed call sounds from the hatch, but sie cannot move from the paralymus spell.

*Ma ga ka si*

*Osi osi.*

The nymph falls back, briefly stunned.

"Stay down!"

Then it rises on tentacles and bursts in speed on the water surface.

*Ma ga ka si*

*Osi osi.*

Namu swirls the spell in her palms and hurls it.

The nymph ducks the awkward spin of Namu's spell that sizzles dead. The nymph deflects the next spell as it bounces several times in its attack. A splash of tentacles on water smothers the next spell, and the ocean gets the brunt of it. The nymph is now skittling onto the tower.

*Maga kasi*

*Osi osi.*

Namu runs and jumps near the edge and releases her spell. The nymph battles in a clash of wills, and Namu is losing. Out of the corner of her eye she sees a kapu—monkey-like with its moon head, rising from the waves. She feels outnumbered.

"You're within range," she hears Maé, but moves close, closer, until she's directly in front of the nymph along *Submerse*'s edge.

"Hold it," cries Maé. "Hold the spell! Create a path and build. Hold it, now drag it back and release!"

"I said stay down!" The spell of destruction disintegrates the nymph while an arrow of flame chars the kapu's pipe nose and yellow-green scales. It roars a giant cry and charges in a flourish of anger or hunger.

*Maga kasi*

*Osi osi.*

Namu's spell fills the kapu's moon head with water, and ruptures it with a ferocious pop that stains the waves yellow-green. The creature drowns.

"That's. An. Overcommit," says Maé.

"One must never summon the spell of destruction unless life depends on it," says Namu. "It depended." Her voice is flat. She doesn't know what to feel. What she knows is that she's not in the mood to argue with her mother.

"An attack can happen quickly," says Maé gently. "Then instinct is what's left." She looks at Namu. "And those beasts will stay down."

"Quiet night, hey?"

"You showed me up today." She studies Namu with pride. "I could do with more practice."

"Did I sustain the challenge?"

"More than, child. And what was that 'own incantation' that I heard?"

"I dreamt my spell."

"Eee, pampula. That is wonderful to hear. What is left for you is to get your own familiar."

"I saw one in the water."

"I always thought it would be a dolphin."

"It wasn't a dolphin"

"What then? A whale?"

"Tilapia."

"A what?"

"So I guess I can't eat fish if my familiar is a tilapia."

"Just like that?"

"I've always wondered about the sweeper. I'm not sure I like it."

"That's the most 'complete' I've ever heard you in words and seen you action, child. You're a short one, but don't you have the leap!"

"I thought you'd reproach me about the sweeper, or not wanting to eat fish, Maé."

"Why in goddess Samaki's name would I do that?"

## Too Much Doom

Maé smiles at the hue of Namulongo's papaya thermals. "Bright like that, no wonder beasts find you."

"Maybe they smell me first."

Their laughter is together.

"Is Bibi going to be alright, Maé?"

"I think so. Sie's a bit sore."

"Oh."

"More hir ego. Sie's more embarrassed than wounded or disappointed about the paralymus spell."

"About being unable to save me?"

"Not like you need saving."

"The attack means that Aunt Umozi knows where we are. She'll send more assassins."

"Her spell of embodiment is clearly more powerful than my woeful demonstration of a bichwa."

"Shall we wait and fight? I am capable now."

"That you are, child." Maé smiles. "But we must drift elsewhere, away from here. It's foolish to wait for more assassins."

#

Namu commands the engine and steers *Submerse* in a new direction, one that might hopefully converge with Auntie Azikiwe's prison. Right now, everything is going on chance.

#

"I miss her," Namu says. She's seated on the ground between her mother's feet.

"I know," says Maé, not asking who. Her fingers pull, tug and weave Namulongo's hair into new plaits.

"Aunt Umozi is too much doom."

"That she is."

A scratching sound in the comms room, then a crackle. Crackle, crackle.

Namu leaps at the same time as her mother.

"Azi!"

"Auntie Azikiwe!"

They snatch the goggles and put them on to a blast of distorted music. A laughing face flickering in and out of the screen. Crimson lips, rows and rows of teeth.

"Got yourself into a pickle." Barking laughter.

"Umozi," spits Maé. "I should have known you'd try to boast. Yet you're hiding behind a mask, too scared to show your true self."

The music rubs and grinds. It cascades into more dissonant laughter. "What if the mask is me, too powerful for you now."

"I'd say you're a bit heavy-footed, and need to get quicker with that spell of embodiment. See how quickly we dispatched your friends."

"It was a small fumble, is all. Next time, it's serious business. I'll not toy with you."

"Eee, pampula. When we catch you, we'll see who's toying."

Aunt Umozi's laughter is more wrong than ever. It's the terrible scream of a burning crowd. "Azikiwe is now my pet."

"Where is she?"

"I moved her to where you'll not find her. You thought you could communicate with her in secret. Well, you bit off a lot to chew. What you need is a solid gut. Because you have nowhere to grow your power."

"That's where you're wrong."

"Of course. Your creation."

"She is my daughter! And she strengthens the quadity!"

The laughter wrapped in high-pitched shrieking is unbearable. A piercing brightness on the screen fills Namu with sounds that yank from her core an internal monologue that is a folding and an absence. It's the sigh of a forgotten sun. It's the reek of a seeping wound. It's the underfoot crunch of a live snail's shell. It's the finger-crush of a squirming worm.

Each sound gets bigger and worse, distinct yet united in its disjointedness. The warm wetness of a wren's tears. The uncomely writhe of a beheaded snake. The crimson sprout of a kudu's vein. The neat doubling of a bub in the tentacles of a receding squid. The century-old rot of a wolffish. The pale mushiness of a stillborn whale. The dreadful gust of a daemon's breath. The dulling flicker in the eyes of a dying magus.

Namu snatches off the goggles at the same time as Maé. They fall into each other's arms in comfort. "That will never sound right at all. Never," says Namu against her mother's chest.

"Child. I have no words for what we've just witnessed."

"In magic, words have power—you said it, Maé."

"My spell doesn't have the journey to do what I want with Umozi."

"I have belief."

"Yes. Now you need *real* belief."

"I've got it."

"It's chained until you know the truth of what happened."

"Then tell me."

"I don't know how to."

"Then you could undo the Fallout."

"Child, you know I cannot put you back."

"Maybe you can."

Maé's grip on Namulongo's shoulder hurts. "Do you understand, *really understand*, what you're asking of me?"

Their eyes are at war. Namu blinks first.

"I guess I need to hear the truth."

"Namulongo, you are more than you know."

"Tell me, Maé, how I am more."

"Will you hear it from Bibi, my child?"

# All Things Are Never Equal

*A sea ghost grips Namulongo's hand in a place of lost and found, and this time there's a dream. The fog wisps in and out of a tale, ebbing and flowing, reacquainting itself with shadow and hiss. The sound and image are an unevenness that's also a myth.*

*Gods are always fighting to determine dominion over others, but this was something else.*

*The story goes that Samaki, the goddess of water, knew that her powers were growing. She was tired of living in the heavens, worn with the fighting, eternally on guard. Her three brothers, Tamoi, Posé and Daga, were flawed. They behaved irrationally, and were always jealous of her strength, though they were more beautiful. Even while Samaki came out strong each battle, she suspected her brothers were uniting in a plot against her.*

*When Tamoi tried to assault Samaki, and put her in a weakened state, that was the last straw. He had mellowed her with wine, crept into her chamber as she slept, but she'd woken. Enraged, she took away his beauty.*

*Tamoi despised his scales and horned nostrils, and now conspired even harder with his brothers Posé and Daga to destroy Samaki. In last resort, Samaki fled from the skies and into waters, where she chose to personify herself as a magus. Her brothers sent assassins, but a goddess as powerful as Samaki was not an easy target to track or kill. But they were getting closer. To mask her trace even more, Samaki split herself into a quadity of magi and sent each on their way. She appointed the first magus as a priestess of rivers and lakes, the second as a priestess of oceans and seas, the third as a priestess of water creatures, and the fourth a priestess of seabeds and islands.*

*Each magus mastered seven spells:*
*The spell of elements: fire, water, air, metal, earth*
*The spell of displacement*
*The spell of embodiment*
*The spell of growth*
*The spell of battle*
*The spell of destruction*
*The spell of creation*
*This last spell, the spell of creation, was genesis. It was one a magus summoned at her hour of death, to ensure continuity. Calling up the spell created a new magus, who came out fully formed. Things stayed this way across generations, a child magus replacing each of the quadity at their dying, and the quad was always four.*

*The time came, and the coven of magi begot Umozi, a priestess of rivers and lakes; Maé, a priestess of oceans and seas; Tatu, a priestess of water creatures; and Azikiwe, a priestess of seabeds and islands.*

*A quadity is perfect, but all things are never equal. There's always a hierarchy. When magi are given to silence, disrespecting the power of dialogue, a challenge will smear its face across amity. Umozi felt shortchanged with her rivers and lakes. She wanted the oceans and seas that were bigger. She craved dominion over water creatures, and also coveted the treasures from islands and seabeds.*

*Fearing the other three magi might grow stronger, Umozi lured Tatu, the most trusting one, to a summit that culminated in a spell of destruction. Umozi overcame Tatu, consumed her powers and her vessel. The killing and swallowing made Umozi exceedingly powerful. But the quadity was broken—three priestesses remained, one a duality.*

*A quad is balance. Killing Tatu was imbalance.*

*Fearing challenge—greed and malice guiding her choices—Umozi knew she could never survive the ordeal of embodying a third priestess: Azikiwe. So she imprisoned Azikiwe. Because Maé's powers to command the seas and the oceans were growing, and her capacity to consume Azikiwe was possible—it didn't matter that Maé intended no such a thing. By imprisoning Azikiwe, Umozi knew that Maé could never create her own duality stronger than Umozi's.*

*The imbalance brought upon the world hurricanes, earthquakes, bushfires, pandemics... And so Maé devised a solution in a spell of creation that summoned a new magus to become the fourth priestess in a quadity that restored harmony. But the new magus was a child, unlearned.*

*Because Maé had invoked the spell before its time.*

*A sea ghost tells this.*

## A Tornado of Flames

The bunk is still warm from Namu's sleep when Maé enters. "It's time for my rotation."

"The idea of sleep has never made you look this happy before, Maé."

"You're always so perceptive, child."

"Those are evasion words, the kind I'd expect from someone who means to tell me nothing."

Maé ruffles Namu's head, snatches her in a quick hug-and-release. "I am happy. Let that be enough."

Namu has an uncanny feel of things. It doesn't always happen, but tonight she has an urgent need to go to the tower. She indulges Maé's carefree mood, as if a burden has been lifted.

"Make me wine while I sleep," says Maé. "I soaked up some maize last night."

#

Namulongo puts the maize in a pestle. She uses a mortar to pound it. She puts the crushed maize in a large clay pot. She plucks four lemons from the veggie patch and squeezes the juice. She slices the rind thin, adds it and the lemon juice to the crush in the pot. She puts in boiling water, adds sugarcane syrup, a scoop of old wine and its ferment, and tightens the lid on the clay pot. The new wine will sit for a week, then be ready for drinking.

But there's more wine on the racks for when Maé wakes.

"That was a nap," protests Namu. "You can sleep more, you know."

"I want to see how the ferment went."

"And you'll see nothing!" Namu slaps her mother from lifting the clay pot's lid. "The wine is brand new." She hands Maé a calabash. "Here, I poured you some from the stock."

"Did you taste it?"

"I am a child."

Maé laughs. "Eee, pampula, these games we play. I didn't hear you bringing up childhood when I offered you cassava wine."

"I like the cassava one better."

"What you need is the right ingredient, and you'll like them all. You won't care if it's maize, cassava or sorghum wine."

#

Up at the tower in the still night, Namu is contemplative.

The big tilapia is out there, circling *Submerse*. It's chittering and beckoning, as if to reassure of its friendliness. Then suddenly it cries and dives below the surface. An albatross glides long and high, riding the ocean wind without a single flap of its giant wings. It makes a sweeping turn, swoops into the waters and soars to the skies with a fish.

Namu looks at the ocean, and appreciates its beauty. And, right now, she *feels* more than sees. What she feels is warmth towards Maé. Now that Namu understands her family story

more, she's become sentimental about Maé's teaching. And
Maé is always teaching, even when she's remonstrating:

*To see the end, look at the beginning.*
*Cultivate the eyes of your magic.*
*You cannot cure spite.*
*To see is to know.*
*Even a fish makes a difference.*
*Be lost to know the way.*
*An attack can happen quickly…*

It all makes sense to Namu now. What doesn't make sense
is the ball of flame now falling from the sky. Entranced, Namu
studies the firewhirl, and falls back when the tornado of flames
the colour of the sun shimmers in a trail and crashes into the
waves.

Namu curses Aunt Umozi and steadies herself for the spell
of battle.

In her mind's eye, as she waits in the terrible silence, she
sees all brutes of monsters: a giant squid that would drown
the vessel; a malevolent water sprite with bad spirits from the
dead; a pregnant gorgon with the hair of venomous snakes; an
ancient bichwa with nothing to lose.

She gazes inwards, sways in the beginning of a chant—

*Namulee, Namulee…* the sea ghost floats and hovers on
the ocean between Namulongo and the grey thing bobbing
on the surface.

Kraa, kra, it cries weakly.

It sounds like a newborn—not that Namu has seen many,
she did see a seal pup once—

Kraa, kra.

Namu drops her stance of attack readiness. She leaps into
the waters and the sea ghost lets her reach the crying thing.
Kraa, kra. Namu floats back with her rescue, and the tilapia is

helping. It nudges them on board with its bottlenose.

The charred bird falls on her wet lap, her thermals sodden.

*Namulee, Namulee...* the sea ghost floats and wraps Namu and the bird in hir fog. Hir heat gently dries Namulongo and the bird that's not a bird, she's now sure. It squeaks weakly, tired, and has feathers now fluffed up on crooked wings. But its face—

Kraa, kra.

"I guess you're sore," says Namu. "And hungry."

Bibi's fog floats them to the cooker, and finally Namu can be astonished. Maé looks up from the diner, where she's seated.

"I don't get it, Maé. Bibi is always so protective of *me*. Sie practically raised me from your meanness."

"And now sie's protecting this one." Maé studies the bird that's not a bird, its wing at an angle.

"Protecting? Fawning!"

Maé tries to touch it but it nips at her. "Look at its face. I think it's a baby phoenix."

"*How* can it be?" Namu studies the ugly thing that's all crooked and depressed, plucking its feathers, crying weakly and refusing to eat.

"Look at its dropping."

"Yes, only one."

Maé picks the dropping, rubs it on the veggie patch soil until it sparkles. "I'd say this is amethyst."

#

"So a ball of flame falls from the sky, it wails like a baby, poops gemstones—and you say it's a phoenix?"

"My best guess," says Maé. "Call it a she, and Bibi loves her."

"Let's call her Phoena."

## Shackery-in-a-Cabin

Phoena's recovery is swift. She fluffs her feathers on Namu's face with glee, her wing less angled. She has a penchant for sunflower seeds, nightshade shoots, the tiny white flowers of the shona cabbage, shrimp and sorghum wine. She steals pecks of wine from Maé's calabash and, having mastered the lid, can push it aside and sully new ferments with a mouth in.

"Let's throw the darn thing back where it came from."

"Auntie Azikiwe said she cast a homing spell. Perhaps Phoena is it?"

"Maybe you have a point. But she's so annoying."

"Don't you wonder how come Bibi is so adoring and protective of it?"

"Still annoying. And it takes some getting used to her face. She reminds me of you as a baby."

"Ugly?"

"No, child. What I mean is that Phoena has a baby face."

#

"Maé! The hatch won't open!"

"Don't be lazy. Just push."

It's an obstruction nobody wants.

"Really, it won't! I've turned the handle, pressed against the hatch. It won't open," says Namu.

They push and heave, fiddle with the lever—and nearly break it.

Maé rolls her eyes and begins to shudder in a chant:

*Inasa bwira*

*Nada ina*

Namulongo gazes inwards, sways in a chant:

*Maga kasi*

*Osi osi.*

Their spells don't go anywhere.

"Do you think Aunt Umozi is behind it?"

"Who else? This is bad. We can't be airlocked. The electrolysis machine can only do so much."

"And the engine?"

"The moon, the stars, remember? Always our friends. Without them—"

"Aunt Umozi has imprisoned us."

"Like she imprisoned Azi. That damned Umozi has thrown peril after peril at us. And now a new obstacle. So straight after the homing—the timing is no coincidence. It means Umozi must be worried that we're winning in our search for Azikiwe."

They look at each other miserably across the dining table in the cooker.

*Namulee, Namulee…* the sea ghost is floating back and forth in agitation.

Namu jumps in excitement. "Perhaps we're close to Auntie Azi!" She looks at Maé. "Why aren't you happy about this?"

"If Umozi is getting worried, she might do worse harm to Azi."

"Maybe my familiar can help."

"You mean the tilapia? You don't know it's your familiar."

True, thinks Namu in misery. The way the fish moves fast in the water, blowing bubbles, all chatty, clicking and whistling, it's probably forgotten its identity and believes it's a playful dolphin.

*Shackery-in-a-cabin!*

They gaze in astonishment at Phoena's new words.

*Shackery-in-a-cabin!*

She's dancing on the table in a funny hop, repeating the words in a bad voice from the roof of her mouth. *Shackery-in-a-cabin.* It's as if she's choking.

"This couldn't possibly get worse," says Maé, just as the lights flicker, dim and black out.

#

The generator groans its last. Now Maé and Namu peer at each other in candlelight.

"We can't run a vessel on spells," says Maé.

"Or find Auntie Azikiwe either."

*Shackery-in-a-cabin!*

"And that stupid bird with its stupid voice won't stop." Maé glares at Phoena.

"It's not a bird."

"Don't you think I know it?" Maé throws her hands in exasperation.

*Shackery-in-a-cabin!*

Phoena begins to stretch and stretch and stretch.

*Namulee, Namulee…* the sea ghost's cry.

"What's happ—" begins Namu.

Maé tackles Namu to the ground away from the phoenix, screams as she burns together with the phoenix that scorches itself in a bright flame of regeneration.

Phoena stands anew in red-gold plumage that reminds Namu of—

"Three words," whispers Maé. "Perfection. Beauty. Paradise."

Lights inside *Submerse* blink awake and in a dazzle. The whole vessel is lit like heaven.

Phoena opens her mouth and doesn't *kraa-kra*, or *shackery-in-a-cabin!* Her song is a fugue of deep and terrible sadness. She sings in staccato of captivity, a city in the sun, and the edge of darkness.

"The sight of you… is a good reason to sing," says Maé. She tries to rise, weakly. Her whole back is naked. Her thermals have melted and joined with skin. She smells of roasted meat. "I just don't know… why you'd choose such… melancholy."

*Namulee, Namulee…*

Maé collapses into the sea ghost's embracing fog.

#

*Who knows the edge of darkness, how or when you might reach it? Is it first light, and then blackness, falling in a pit full of serpents that stare intently at you, flickering tongues before they strike? Is it an abyss that goes and goes deeper inside a pit that is bottomless, and it's the belly of a basilisk or a carnivorous eel, or the drowning waters of a beastly crocodile trapping you in a killing grip? Is it a feeling like you're on fire, and excruciatingly so, and you're parched and starved and gobbled in gloom? And your spirit is lonesome, your memory smoggy, and your tomorrow smothered for breath?*

*A sea ghost asks this.*

## Command the Vessel

Bibi's fog helps with the healing. Namulongo can only guess at treating the burns. First, she cools Maé with a wet compress. It soothes the blisters. She keeps them moist, changing the plant dressing every now and then with a potion of aloe vera, sunflower oil and honey to reduce crust formation.

"Can't I break the blisters?"

"Don't," whispers Maé. Her face is scarred along the cheek that was nearest to the flames. "It'll bring infection." Maé forbids Namu from using a spell. "A phoenix has its own powers…" she explains. "Gods forbid if you mixed those with incantation."

"It's me who took Phoena in—I feel bad."

"No. It's my fault…" says Maé.

Phoena must feel more guilty. The moroseness in her lilted song makes Namu wish for *kraa-kra*, or *shackery-in-a-cabin!* She doesn't tell Maé this. She doesn't tell her mother about Phoena's second regeneration either, how she burned up and rebirthed to a bigger and more perfect self, more red and gold plumage, but sing-wailing a melancholier composition that stopped the moon from shining.

The hatch is fixed, now opening to the surface.

Namu finishes putting on a new skin dressing of crushed aloe in banana leaves. "Maybe we shouldn't be flogging ourselves," she says quietly. "There's not much merit in it."

"I took a beat too long, though I knew the phoenix was transforming, and what happens when it does."

"You're a poor patient at best. It's hell when you moan."

"Sleeping all the time on my belly. Kill me already. Where is the quality of life?"

"I can turn you on your side. It's healed properly."

"No."

"Accept when you need help," Namu says firmly. She puts a calabash to Maé's mouth. "Drink this."

"Is it poison?"

"It's green tea and black pepper. It will cut the swelling."

"Now you're a herbalist?"

"What you need next is wild lettuce tea that will put you to sleep. Because I can't tolerate you. Now take a nap."

"You take a nap."

#

Namu busies herself with chores. She inspects the hull, angles the periscope, scrapes scum off the shower and checks the oxygen chamber.

Phoena is crooning a pitiful melody. It's a song that's a fugue of breaking glass. It seems to be about flowers—how they wink when you're not looking. How their snow-white petals are suspicious about ebony cats but adore spectral monsters, especially those that creep when you turn your back. How conspirators visit your nightmares and morning news, all undrawn to scale.

Namu compacts the trash and ejects it from the watertight exit in the hull. She forces away the urge to paint, because the tough steel of *Submerse* is good as new since Phoena's transformation restored the lights. The engine, the fins, the propellers are all running to perfection. What's interesting is Tila—Namu has named the so-called familiar—always in the eye of the periscope.

#

Namu wants Maé to get better, but today she's running a temperature. Namu is fatigued and sore from lying on the cold steel floor. But she pushes herself onwards making fish soups for her patient. It's almost contradictory, somewhat carnivorous, that she would have a tilapia for a familiar, but still prepare fish. She makes stock of the baby bluefin, curries the cod, steams the flounder, crushes the bass into a pottage, stir-fries the halibut.

She tends to the bees, brings new flowers for a fresh batch of pollen and spiced honey. She cultivates the veggie patch, prunes the shona cabbage, shakes out the amaranth seeds. She crushes them and bakes bread. She's exhausted! But makes a pickle. Takes octopus from freezer bags in the reefer—residues of the sweeper's last harvest eons ago—Namu no longer harvests fish. Chops the octopus into a tiny pot, adds salt, water, chilli, oregano and sunflower oil, and seals the jar.

The aroma of the rising bread silences Phoena's glum singing and brings her to the cooker. Namu makes a sauce of red eggplant—it's bigger, more crimson than a tomato, and cooks well in a stew. They wash it down with baobab juice.

#

Maé is worse. "Let me close my eyes just a moment," she whispers, when Namu tries to feed her cowpea gruel.

"I don't want to do it alone," Namu finally breaks. Her voice wobbles. A lone tear trails her cheeks.

Maé tries to smile encouragement. Her once even face is gaunt, ashen. "I must rest, build my strength."

"I can't do it…"

"Yes… you can." Maé puts her fingers on the back of Namu's hand. "*Submerse* is yours now." She smiles again weakly. "You'll make it."

"I need you, Maé."

"Take us to Azikiwe. She needs us."

"But Maé—"

"This is your go, child. Stop hesitating." Her eyes twinkle in a hint of mischief. "You'll be fine. You and that curselet Phoena, and that tilapia familiar of yours."

She closes her eyes to the blanket of Bibi's fog.

## Even a Fish Makes a Difference

Maé scrunches her face, pushes away the bowl. "So bitter. You burnt the cabbage."

"I didn't."

"Then you're determined to poison me."

"Earlier, didn't you want to die, Maé?"

"Nonsense. And what's Phoena doing here? Too bright." She looks at the phoenix. "You don't belong here. Go to the city of the sun or the edge of darkness you've been mauling us with in song."

"That's just mean, Maé. Leave Phoena alone."

"Maybe I should get up." She starts to rise.

"You'll do no such thing." Namu pushes her back into the bunk. "Keep up the ungratefulness and I'll embody you with a spell that will sleep you for eons."

"With both of us eternally sleeping, who'll rescue Azi?"

"Then I'll summon paralymus and abandon you for eons."

Maé succumbs. "Why use a spell of battle when we're not even fighting? Besides, the effects of a paralymus spell are only temporary."

"Before I'm done with you, it'll feel like eons. Now shut up, woman, and sleep."

"Eee, pampula. No. Stop racing ahead of yourself. I gave you command of the vessel, not of my body."

#

Namu grinds more amaranth seeds and is baking muffins when her mother wanders into the cooker.

"Looks like you're out of trouble, Maé."

"What's happening?"

"I take it you're not asking about the muffins." Namu takes her mother's hand, guides her to the tower. "We've been moving everywhere, reaching nowhere. But now we have a compass."

"And it is?"

"Come, look through the periscope."

Maé looks. "I see a fish."

"*That's* the compass."

"Is that your plan: follow the tilapia?"

"It's no ordinary fish. Tila has been beckoning me to follow and, finally, I listened."

"I hope something more solid than a fish guided your decision on a journey that not only affects us, but Azi's fate."

"Didn't you say even a fish makes a difference?"

"I am turning this vessel."

"And Phoena, Phoena! What have you noticed?"

"I'll avoid the phoenix at all costs."

"Once we started steering towards Tila, Phoena stopped singing those deep and terribly sad songs."

"So she's your familiar too?"

"You're annoyed with me."

"Let me think about that for a short time and I'll confirm with you just how enraged I am by your foolishness."

## A Child, Unlearned

"What's that?" Namu points.

"It's a beach," says Maé.

It's as if someone has made a deal with the gods of weather. Though it's night, outside is bright and white. Namu blinks. If this is the edge of darkness, she honestly doesn't mind it.

"It's land," she cries. "Land!"

"I feel foolish for letting you convince me to follow the tilapia."

"And the phoenix. We knew the journey was wrong every time Phoena went maudlin in song, and we changed steer."

A mud-coloured guillemot peers low with its white face, lets out a high-pitched pipe call.

*Namulee, Namulee…* the sea ghost's animated cry.

"Can't you see, Maé? Phoena and Tila have led us to Auntie Azikiwe. Aunt Umozi must have hidden her here, where we'd never think to search."

"I don't know—"

"Look at Tila, somersaulting in glee. Auntie's here. She must, oh, please, she must be here."

"Is it possible?" whispers Maé.

Staccato piping, then a tremulous whistle from the guillemot.

Phoena begins to stretch. But rather than explode in a new scorcher, then a paradise of plumage, she flies out from the tower in a dazzle of beauty. Her hair cascades in the colour of the sun. Her trail of shimmer sweeps the skies.

Namu cups her hand and calls out from the tower. "Come with?"

"Where did you learn a phrase like that?" She looks at the beach. "Hmrrph. Come with! *Submerse* will have to wait here. Think you can swim out there?"

"Let's, quick Maé."

Namu drags out from the flow and ebb of the tide and onto land. Her phoenix is in a glow overhead. Namu looks backwards. The vessel that is her house disappears behind the ocean. The water wears the pale blue of a pearl she's never seen. A beach dazzles with glistening sand. She sprints to catch up with Maé. Trees of a velvet green remind her of eating avocados. And are those coconut trees? Or palm trees, floppy ears defending their nuts? Here, the call of birds is louder. Merry whistles, chirpy flutes. One bird is singing a cheery squeaker-ree, squeaker-ree. Perhaps they are seasonal, those flowers on a brush. Coned petals in a flaming orange speak the language of this world.

Maé is walking towards a dilapidated cabin on the beach. A long-legged bird with blue-black feathers and a red beak gingerly prowls the beach, unperturbed by the tourists' presence. It's a kind of bird Namu has never seen.

Namu kicks off her shoes and races barefoot. Sand grains tickle between her toes. She avoids a rock, sprints past a brown man walking his mud-faced dog that's otherwise all white. The dog notices her, the man barely registers her. The dog lopes, ears flat. Its tail wags. It barks and leaps at the bird that takes flight.

The shack is a pitiful array the size of a pit latrine. It's tinier than the facilities on *Submerse*. It's near a three-stone hearth all ashed—someone cooked a meal on it centuries ago. Namu picks a rock and approaches the padlocked hut.

"That won't do. The lock is enchanted."

Maé rolls her eyes and begins to shudder in a chant. Nothing happens.

Namulongo drops the rock. She gazes inwards, sways in a chant. The padlock bangs against the wood. Nothing else happens.

"Auntie Azikiwe, if you're in there help us."

A groan.

"Azi!"

"Auntie!"

"Don't make a meal of it," says a melodious, but weak, voice. "Just save me."

"That's like it," says Maé. "You went quiet too long after our last communication."

"Umozi moved me from my submersible to this horrid cabin. Forgive me that she didn't think it was a good idea to install comms. Get me out!"

"We must spell together, Auntie," cries Namu.

Maé rolls her eyes and shudders in her chant:

*Inasa bwira*

*Nada ina.*

Namulongo gazes inwards, sways in a chant:

*Maga kasi*

*Osi osi.*

A hiss from inside the hut:

*Rozi tasi*

*Navi dato.*

The padlock snaps, and Auntie Azikiwe falls out of the door, gasping for air.

She coughs. "It was a coffin in there! I was better in the submersible before that fool snatched me."

"You survived Umozi."

"I barely scraped through." Delicate reed, musical notes in her voice. "When she found out we were talking, she brought me to this place without technology. Called it my eternal tomb, that no-one would find me. But you did." She casts her green-blue eyes at her rescuers. "Thank you." The fern in her green hair is not bouncy on her shoulders. It's parched. Her skin that looked yellow from their control chamber is here a smooth caramel.

"Your eyes—innocent, big and curious—just as I knew," Auntie Azikiwe says. "Don't stare at me, chile, like you're witnessing a ghost."

She's lean and lanky for one with child, a sinewy frame, famished a long time. Yet she wears a sweet smell of passionfruit or melon as she envelops Namu in her arms.

"You've got a smell on you, girl."

"There's a story," laughs Maé.

"The smell is jungle," says Namu. "Now I can be a land voyager."

"And a water voyager," says Auntie Azikiwe. "You belong to land and sea. Or land and sea belong to you." She straightens and studies Maé. "You look… business."

"I am."

"Is that unusual?"

"Very. You look… trouble."

"Oh, I feel worse. But maybe look better than you." Auntie Azikiwe touches the scarring along Maé's cheek. "What happened?"

"Your homing spell."

They laugh, embrace.

Namulongo looks at them: Maé's even face, Auntie Azikiwe's high cheekboned one. She feels overwhelmed. Now that it's happened, she's struggling to accept they're finally together. It's almost a dream, one too good to indulge.

"Now what's this about burns and homing spells?"

"That phoenix you sent. Up, there she is."

"Her name is Phoena," says Namulongo.

"A phoenix? I thought you tried to cook the tilapia and it bested you."

"I did no such thing. Why would I want to cook a familiar?"

"A familiar? The tilapia is the homing spell."

"What?" cry Namu and Maé in unison. They look upwards at the phoenix.

Namulongo recalls what Maé said about being gifted with fire. It isn't a fire dragon.

"My guess, chile," says Auntie Azikiwe, kneeling to face level, "is that Phoena is the familiar you've so badly been waiting for." She looks at Maé. "Now one or both of you—do something. I'm hungry enough to eat a school of wolffish."

"Namulongo can do it."

"Can she, really?"

Namu stretches a hand, fells two coconuts with a chant. They topple in turn and land at her feet.

"You might still need those toes," says Maé.

These coconuts are giant compared to the miniature ones Namulongo knows.

"You have a good core, the way you belt out that chant," says Auntie Azikiwe.

Namu pulls the fibre from the kernel, cracks the shell with

a rock. "It's a fresh young one. Take it, Auntie. To the richness of the ocean."

"And the strength of belief," whispers Auntie Azikiwe.

She drinks the coconut water in hungry swallows as Maé prepares the second nut. Auntie Azikiwe holds out the nut to Namu. "For you now."

"You drink it."

"Chile."

Namu tastes the sweet and sour nut in the translucent coconut water. She uses her finger to scoop the soft white gelatine. "Here, Auntie."

The second coconut is older, its white meat crunchier. But its aroma is sweeter, and munching its white flesh gives creamier milk.

"I needed this. What I could do with more is some soft stone to chew." Auntie Azikiwe pats her swelling belly. "Maybe you can magic it."

Maé's look has changed.

"Say it," says Auntie Azikiwe. "It's loud in your silence, that thing you say about the spell of creation—how it's forbidden."

"There's obligation," says Maé in a kind voice. "I'm not angry, Azi. Just thankful."

"You always put your own spin on matters." She stills the hand on her belly. "You understand it'll be a child, unlearned?"

"Of course."

## Denouement

"What's your prognosis?" They are sitting around a hearth fire, the three of them together with Bibi and Phoena. The fire is more for sentiment than a need for light or warmth. Auntie Azikiwe looks at Namulongo, then Maé.

"The early signs are good," says Maé. "What more would anyone want? The child can guide a spell beautifully and smother a kraken."

"Amazing."

"She responds to instruction or reprimand as quickly as you can say it."

"Really?"

"No."

"I'm right here, you know," says Namu.

"It's good to see that you and your mother are getting along," says Auntie Azikiwe.

"Oh, we're feeling each other along the edges," says Maé.

"I see. Protective as ever, clucky. What's that saying about a mother hen?"

"Mother hen nothing." Maé rises. "Are we rescuing you or not?"

"No need to make a crowd of it."

"A crowd, or an audience?"

"And the difference?" says Auntie Azikiwe. She looks at Maé, who doesn't answer. "I thought so."

Laughter on the horizon cuts off Maé's reply. The laughter is dissonant, always wrong.

"Looks like Umozi is finally here," says Auntie Azikiwe. "I told you she was using me as bait."

"And she can fly," says Namulongo in wonderment. "Like an evil lightning bird."

"She's mightier than ever, but will never rest until she takes our power or destroys us all," says Maé.

A terrible howl fills Namu with misgiving, fear and dread. The sound is worse in the open than it was on the screen. A face flickers in and out of the sky. But what comes out of the most blackened clouds are not crimson lips and a gnash of teeth: it's a coffee-skinned woman with a petite petal mouth.

"She's very deceptive," says Auntie Azikiwe. "Be careful."

Together, they watch the descent. Umozi floats to her feet. She has satin skin and golden-brown eyes. Her smooth face, the shape of an egg, is framed in a blue-black fringe, and a sweep of long, slippery hair roped in braids.

Wearing such a kindly face, Aunt Umozi looks like a magus that Namu—if she didn't know different—might want to acquaint with.

Auntie Azikiwe touches Namu's chin. She looks into her eyes. "You have a big role, chile. You understand this?"

Namu nods.

"She runs and flies," says Maé impatiently. "Of course, she understands."

"I have belief," says Namu.

"And courage?" asks Auntie Azikiwe.

"Courage also."

"Good."

"To be clear, I'll dishearten you both with a reminder," says Maé. "A quadity is never five. One of us will die today—"

"And I know just who. She needs to give me back the submersible and my damn whale!" says Auntie Azikiwe.

"… and if you care about that baby—" Maé looks at the sky, "maybe it's better that you don't fight."

"The baby is kicking for battle."

"In which case, it had better know how to spell."

Auntie Azikiwe's glance at Maé is quizzical. "I've never known you to give in that easy."

Maé shrugs. "There's a lot on the line," she says. "And I've never known myself to shy from help."

"Then let's see who gets first hands on evil."

"First, I'd better tell this one something." Maé looks at Namulongo. "That out there is evil. Don't just run at it."

No-one laughs, the tension taut. A big wind swirls around their positions: heads tilted, knees bent, palms attentive to spelling. Phoena swoops down in a blaze and joins them. Her ruby eyes are fierce. Bibi's fog is full of menace.

Umozi walks towards them in a graceful flow. She breaks into a sprint in a stream of braids. Her soft brown eyes are kinder than ever.

"Don't forget just how potent she is," hisses Auntie Azikiwe.

Maé rolls her eyes and begins to shudder in a chant.

Namulongo gazes inwards, sways in a chant.

Auntie Azikiwe glares, hisses her chant.

A trio of spells falls out in unison, in a language of Babel:

*Inasa bwira*

*Nada ina.*

~
*Maga kasi*
*Osi osi.*

~
*Rozi tasi*
*Navi dato.*

A whirling hurricane gulps the four magi into the gut of a fierce battle.

THE LUMINESCENT GHOST DRINKS

## An Urge for Words and Silence

Coincidence was never pure. The goddess keeled and gave a loud cry. She clutched her side, half-stuttered in agony. The invisible saw, also silent inside, hacked from her gut, through her viscera and trembled all the way with scorch and slice to the edges of her heart.

It was pain of a kind she'd known but once before—when she understood that an intimate part of her had died, but she didn't know how. It was the death of her self or child self, yet not. It was an ilk of torment that first cut, bearing terrible heat in each slice, then collapsed in a false sense of calm. Something moved, altered, then shattered in a fireball that flung her with such force she found herself in a strange world with a swift-flowing creek humming over pebbles.

Ducks floated on the bluest water, but they were smaller than her ducks in the Savanna with its sweep of golden grasslands awash in eternal light. She relied on immortality, being all-knowing in the skies. But this! What was left over from the explosion was less dramatic. Soon as she could straighten she studied a sign that said this was a town called Mottram.

No doubt she was on Earth.

She followed the creek down a mountain until she found a path to the town centre lined with shopfronts, some open, some closed. This one sold candy. That one sold coffins.

By coincidence—which was a deceptive thing to a goddess—everyone wore brown overalls and a good number of them seemed to farm grey donkeys, as they were sitting on, walking alongside or hauling them. And they were laden with sacks of meat, fruit and vegetables.

She followed the rear of the donkey trail and arrived at an open market. The air smelt of barbeque. It appeared the townsfolk were holding a fair where a gap-toothed man played something called a banjo and children wearing knee-length socks—all rainbow—hopped, clapped and galloped to its lost music.

The children said she had a way of walking up quietly. No-one questioned the goddess' presence—it seemed a natural acceptance that affirmed itself when a little girl brought her flowers full of sweetness and brine. The braid-haired child curtsied and vanished before the goddess could think to say the right thing. One woman shimmied close and twirled her, twirled her. Another woman in a flowing dress handed her a plate, and that was that for any more thought of saying the right thing. The goddess found herself with a glass of wine that was nowhere near marula but, oh, so heady!

Despite the music's noise, and the embellishments of its making, the goddess felt so calm, surrounded in uncomplicatedness and kindness that seemingly spread from the mountains to her soul, she wanted to throw off her robe and walk around naked.

But this was not her calling, not that which summoned her. Her wings found urgency and she unfolded them. She flew over a peat swamp, then brick houses, past a trio of hillocks and over a place called Fish Creek that seemingly wrote itself with sombre credentials that tugged at her longing for home.

She contemplated her three sons and lost daughter, and how it went so wrong.

#

Light rain fell at dawn. She was alone, yet connected to a multitude in sentience. She felt each sum of self's love, heartache, loss, even rage. They soared with her together, yet absent.

Darn it, she was alone.

Torn between the urge for words and silence. She flew, walked, looked, felt. She, they. Each of them carrying some disarray, a place to go… never reaching… in a pattern of their own making. Each bore a great desire, wanderlust or restlessness for something, and it created an inner absence the goddess understood too well.

But it was her daughter Samaki the goddess felt the loudest—at first as a singularity, then in scatter. Sometimes the multiplicity was up to four, across oceans and seas, rivers and lakes, seabeds and islands, sometimes in sea monsters. When she felt that terrible wounding, the saw that sliced and scorched, the multiplicity diminished, and she understood loss as she did now.

## The Hurricane Groaned

Namulongo doesn't talk much, but she has a grudge. And grief. She plans revenge in her spells. How she'll first tear Aunt Umozi limb by limb in a spell of battle, then cremate her alive in a spell of destruction.

She feels confused, like a new ghost that hasn't found its words, let alone a niche as it drifts across life and nonlife. Is she a scare ghost? A melancholy ghost? A vengeance ghost? Her unpreparedness suggests she could never be a guardian ghost, just a burnt one lingering in unrequited love, no open windows, all doors hardened. She peers for a passage to light from her darkness, but there's no silver lining in the blackness of doom's ferry approaching in shapes and on time, which is how she feels ever since—

It is only days from when that terrible battle happened on a beach and took Maé. Even Umozi appeared stunned by her triumph, as a spell of destruction incinerated Maé—no ashes to bury. Umozi's brown eyes widened in shock, then dismay. She hurled herself to the skies in a whirling hurricane that groaned.

*Namulee, Namulee…*

Alongside the luminescent ghost's mourning and the

phoenix's scream, Namulongo heard Auntie Azikiwe's guttural cry, or perhaps it was her own, and then her auntie's hands were under her arms, hauling Namulongo away from the beach, away, away… across its white wash and onto *Submerse*.

#

Without Maé, the underwater home is a tomb. Namu gazes out to the ocean. Each tide is a slit on her throat, each splashing quiet but potent. She has no desire to swim—when she tries, the water's touch is a nightmare that consumes.

Namu is a ghost this moment, confused and focused. Everything that put her into this world from her creation has lost meaning. She is the threshold of herself, cold, removed. Splashed with loss. No matter how forward she moves, she feels stepped back, turned around, gasping for… she doesn't know what. Her eyes brim with memory—what is her mettle, and how to find it for a life lived backwards? The best trips start at sea, if she could just but smell the depth of its freedom.

"Eat, chile," Auntie Azikiwe pleads. "I can cast a spell of embodiment that might help a little, bring her memory in a bird or a fish—perhaps in Tila?"

They are up on the vessel's surface, Auntie Azikiwe holding out a steaming bowl of peanut and eggplant soup, but it turns Namulongo's stomach. She shakes her head. Auntie Azikiwe joins her in the leg dangle, feet touching the water.

In silence, her auntie's stomach swollen to bursting, they watch the fish that thinks it's a dolphin, clicking, whistling and doing somersaults in the waves.

## No Tim Tams, Please

The goddess focused and willed herself to be. She followed where the signal was strongest, and was astonished to land outside a commonplace building whose entrance door swung inwards. A sign said: *Waterman*.

"What's going on, mate?" the man at the counter said, as if they were life chums. He splashed a glass with ale from a tap and pushed it to the goddess where she stood by the counter. "Bit early, but hey." He laughed.

"She was here," the goddess said.

"We get all kinds," the man said, and busied himself shining glasses with a towel. "The crowds be here this arvo. Prelims." He nodded at a box with a woman talking in it. "Footy," he added at her raised brow. "You from Woop Woop?"

"Savanna," she said. "I'm looking for my daughter."

"Genius. Good luck finding 'er." He looked at the goddess. "She wanna be found?" He understood her silence. "They're funny ones, hey? Children. Don't matter it's a lass or a lad."

He entered the kitchen, returned with a plate. "You better eat then, need the strength. On the house."

"What is it?"

"Burger with the lot," he said. "Beetroot too."

"Do you have a name?" she asked when she swallowed.

"It's not Gum Leaf. But they call me Little Timmy."

"Does that work for you?"

"I don't like Tim Tams."

"I'm Goddess Mother," she said.

"Bloody oath."

She looked around. "Something happened here, I can feel it. I can also feel a beach, strongly."

"Won't be finding one here." He stacked dirty glasses into an artefact that seemed to be a washer. "You smell good."

She laughed. "I make an effort."

He laughed with her, his hearty roar. "Born smelling that good, you can be a goddess mother all you like."

"It's an evening fragrance of devil's thorn," she said.

"Won't be asking about the shimmer and dance in that blue hair."

"Don't."

They shared a comfortable silence, until finally she said, "I had better get moving." She held his quiet gaze. "Thank you."

"No worries, mate."

"I will see you around."

"You reckon—where you off to?"

She smiled, copied how he spoke. "Get me head right."

#

She was a goddess, but it was other gods who touched her, even just in passing. Like the time one brushed her elbow in the lift of the Umqombothi, a hotel bigger than her palace and it had ebony windows that you could look out of but nobody from outside saw in. He was a bellboy in this world, climbed her up to a penthouse. Helped her as if he knew her. It was the eyes that told her his godliness. A swirl tumbling inside. And the deep listening—despite her silence. "Do you believe in coincidences?" he said.

She found another one under the strobe lighting of a discotheque whose dance floor was swollen with bodies. The new god was a DJ who waved, bought her drinks that fizzed and smoked, tasted of spiced pavlova flowers. This new god, a woman… it was as if they were childhood friends even if they'd just met.

"Look at the night!" the god said.

"Why?" the goddess asked.

She found another in velvet green wilderness, trees taller than she knew. He made several trips, hauling tarpaulins—she knew them from the swimming pool when she stayed at the hotel tiered like a krantz aloe cake. She'd marvelled at how resourceful humans were, yet so reckless. They cut holes on the roof of a building to make a tiny lake with a shimmering bed, wrapped it at night with canvas. There was a creep about the place with this god, and she couldn't put a finger on it. So she stayed hidden as the god hauled something towards a crimson-stained river, and swore she saw movement, perhaps a wobble, then a groan inside the tarp.

She wondered how the gods here were so many, unburied. Now she wondered if Little Timmy was also a god.

#

She found a beach where magic happened. She touched the water. Samaki was here. She looked out to the horizons and felt a pull, intense, to enter the water.

She swam out and found another beach where death happened.

# A New Magus Is Born

The baby arrives quietly.

*Namulee, Namulee…* the sea ghost wraps him in hir fog.

Phoena croons lullabies that put him to sleep in a cot with a smile. His name is Imani. He has tight black hair and Maé's eyes, ebony pearls that glint silver.

"You will teach the new chile."

"Auntie?"

"His magic is inside. He is a magus too. But he must learn it."

#

The view wasn't a painting or a stream. It was a present that was a past. Why were they? Here was family—her only duty to keep it safe. A giant fog was rolling, and it ran afoul. She questioned her perspectives, the trickery of thinking. But she was prepared to grimace if it brought back watercolours across the horizon.

The goddess drank to small hearts full of dreams.

She had failed Samaki—now she drank to never be detached from anything.

## A Multiplicity, and Death

She grew out of wishes when her children didn't fit anymore. She'd worn them like cloaks, now they snatched away when she reached to enter her hand into a sleeve. She was curling into a cape when she forgot why she was there, how it made a difference and where to find a rune that would return her children back to their stars.

When Samaki left, Posé, Tamoi and Daga became increasingly unruly. They were her sons, yet she could not contain them.

But there was hope still, she felt it. Hope in a new—

Birth.

Her longing finally guided her to a vessel under the ocean. She stepped through, not needing doors to enter. Compartments and compartments segmented with tight corners.

*Namulee, Namulee…* a luminescent fog approached in a sway. Sie didn't seem menacing. Then a ruby-eyed phoenix, blaze in its red-gold plumage, appeared. It bowed its head, as if in worship, equally unharming.

"Goddess Mother," said a sweet-voiced woman as if in song.

The goddess studied the high cheekbones, the blue-green pearls in the eyes. She recognised this stranger whose slippery hair was Samaki's. "You know me?"

"Yes, Goddess Mother." The lilt in her voice was a song of wind and dawn.

The goddess touched the woman's face. "I see her likeness." She turned to the curious-eyed child—about nine cycles tall— who had appeared wearing a papaya-hued thermal suit. The girl gawped, no doubt confounded by the goddess' engulfing shimmer that revealed itself to those who knew her. "Come to me."

The child approached. She smelt of rich salt. The goddess touched her face. "And in you, I see her likeness. Samaki's." She turned to the woman. "How?"

"I am Azikiwe," the woman said. "And this is Namulongo, gifted with fire. She is Maé's daughter. We are part of a quadity of magi that Samaki created."

The goddess understood. "A multiplicity?"

"Yes."

"I felt—" the goddess struggled with the word. "A passing."

Azikiwe touched her gently. "There have been deaths. And births."

"I think you had better tell me from the start."

The girl Namulongo began to cry.

# The Awakening

*Maga kasi*
  *Osi osi.*
  Flame bursts on the wicks in the chapel's candles. Namulongo kneels by the altar. Etiquette proposes that children do not die before their parents. It's doom to put grief in a mother's soul halfway through living. But what about a child's soul?

The chapel, in its disquiet on the lower level of *Submerse* with an altar and a grimoire on Namu's lectern, is arranged. Flowers smelling the citrusy hint of rose dandelion are reminiscent of a remarkable yet bittersweet span lived and unlived. The baby Imani reminds Namu of life, yes, of life— when all she has is death, but it's a death along the inevitability of etiquette's poetry that will not bring her mother back.

#

Namulongo is out on the bridge. She faces the water for the first time since—

She turns away from it, naked. She flicks backwards in a dive. Her fingertips glide in first, tight in a clean arrow, head and shoulders following in a crisp entry without breaking the water's surface.

## A Darkening Horizon

The goddess studied the child playing with a fast-moving fish in the water. Occasionally, Namulongo clasped its white and black belly and flipped onto its back to ride it.

The goddess wondered about her dream when, finally, she could sleep on a shared bunk bed still warm with the heat of the girl and her handwoven thermals the colour of love.

"Maé made them," Namulongo had wistfully said.

Everything faded in that dream, and the goddess zipped between now and never, seeing an unknown hero/ine walking the water's surface. It was unclear if it were a man or woman. She ran to catch up but never reached the figure out front, always, always at the same distance, and leaving familiar footsteps. Appearing then disappearing in a split. Nothing of consequence happened, just a haloed hero/ine—never turning—strolling out of reach and pouring through walls, mountains, walking, walking to an endless distance. The goddess tried but failed to remember what else she must do other than follow or try to catch up before the next hour arrived. Then she woke.

Now she looked up to the greying horizon and, for the first time, understood fear.

It felt as if her sons were coming. Posé—she could never put anything past him. It didn't matter how they might track a split quadity of magi. But perhaps it was her trail that led them here.

\#

They sat round the table, inside the cooker that was both a kitchen and a diner. Bees hummed in a nearby honeycombed hive. Azikiwe nursed baby Imani.

"He will settle well in Savanna," the goddess said.

"Is that a question?" asked Azikiwe.

"No." The goddess studied Namulongo, whipping up fresh baobab soup and cassava pies.

Namulongo plated the food.

"To the richness of the ocean," she said.

"And the strength of belief," the goddess and Azikiwe answered in unison.

The girl was good in the cooker—when she wasn't brooding, or making plant dye for her quill pen, or sitting cross-legged in the chapel on a carpet of antelope skin, writing with her quill radiant-coloured hexes and divinations into her grimoire of tempered bark.

The goddess spoke to no-one in particular. "This is not your world, and Savanna is humming for—" she sought a word, "good," she finally said.

Azikiwe said nothing.

"Have you seen the sky?" the goddess asked.

"Looks filthy," said Azikiwe. It was fogged.

"Are you worried about it?"

"Not especially. Why—you think Umozi is coming?"

"I think it's Posé, Tamoi and Daga. I created them in my own image, but I cannot shape their passions. Such is their hatred for Samaki, they will find you and the girl and the bub, and they will find Umozi."

"I have you," said Azikiwe, and glanced at Phoena, Namu and the baby. "And them."

"It is not enough, and Imani's magic is not ready."

"Then what? Give up?"

"You must unite to overcome evil's might."

"Including Umozi's?"

"We must find Umozi in order that you make peace. Did you not tell of a quadity of magi, strongest in unity? You must battle as one."

"Even the baby?"

"Especially the baby."

"Why?" the curious one, Namulongo, asked. She was warming to the goddess and let her plait her braids.

"Because magic is strongest at its purest," the goddess said.

"Ga ga ga ga," the baby gurgled.

Then began the rain, an endless downpour.

## Together They Are

Goddess Mother's inner 'signal' guides their search. "It's a feeling," she says, "and I trust it because it helped me find you. Now it will lead us to Umozi."

Namulongo wishes it were a homing spell—like the one Auntie Azikiwe cast through Tila—rather than a feeling.

They rise to the surface at sundown. They arrive at a crag. They step outside *Submerse* to a storm. Angry drops large as fists lash at them.

"Are you sure?" asks Auntie Azikiwe, a musical reed in her voice.

"More than ever," Goddess Mother says.

They swim out against the deluge towards a cliff and tumble down a howling waterfall. Phoena blazes overhead, the baby enfolded in her wings.

Namu slips out of the water's edge as it spits her sodden onto the beach. She claws to her feet and slaps across the rocks. Her grudge slips out and moulds with her grief, stamping with her all the way into a sea cave that echoes her bellow.

At first the loudness of the ravenous animal rushing in sound from her stomach is fluid and shrill. "Uuuuuuuuu!" Then the beast rolls, full of darkness. "Uuuuuuuuu!" The sound gets deeper, broken in staccato. "Uuu-uuu-uuu." It's the dissolving grunt of an animal, never figurative. It longs, belongs. "Uuu. Uuu." It needs to eat again. "Uuu."

She hurls herself at a woman in her own image sat on the ground, dead skin in unspoken words, illegible details. But a force holds her mid-leap. She tosses a fist that should have connected with Umozi's jaw, dislodged it to the ground. But her knuckles refuse to reach Umozi's face. She swings a kick straight from the hip, and it's stronger than an ostrich's killer one. But nothing—the force holds her back and her kick doesn't reach its mark. Namu squints at Goddess Mother whose brightness—even from a distance—is a pulling, a passion that draws rage back into itself. Namu throws back her head and wrenches out a long howl. "A-ooooo! O-woooo!" Its low pitch comes and goes in chorus, ending in a series of *ruff ruffs* until only gasps remain.

Goddess Mother releases the force and Namu crumples to the ground. The swallowing intensity of the goddess mother's luminosity is calming.

"There's been enough bloodshed, no?" Goddess Mother's voice comes from somewhere, inside, outside.

"We were just having… words," says Namulongo.

But she's calmer.

There is Umozi—not inside her titanium vessel, or Azikiwe's stolen submersible. She's in a cave behind the waterfall. It is crawling with death beetles, spilling in and out of a writhing serpent speared by a fallen stalactite. Umozi is knees up on the ground, arms folded around herself. Her once blue-black hair is ashen.

Namu understands the futility of what she had intended before Goddess Mother intervened—where's the fun in attacking *that*? What vengeance could it be for Maé?

There was no dignity in rage directed at one so helpless. The knowing restores Namu somewhat, and she rises to her feet. Her dripping scurries away salamanders.

As if sensing the inner change, Umozi turns to look at Azikiwe, then Namulongo.

Azi steps over cavefish swimming in a thin pool near stalactites fanged as blades.

*Rozi tasi*
*Navi dato.*

Auntie Azikiwe's spell of elements whistles and their clothes are no longer drenched.

Now Namu feels disquiet rather than hatred. She has processed her grief, and rage would be useless on the Umozi blinking at them, her clothes tattered. Nothing is potent about her—this is not the aunt who walked towards them in a graceful flow on a beach and cast the spell that decimated Maé.

It's a smog of the Umozi whose eyes widened in shock, then dismay, at her unconscionable deed. The same Umozi who flung herself with an abysmal moan to the darkened skies and roiled away in a tempest. Since that fateful day—when Azi was still pregnant with Imani, and now he was born—it appears Umozi's shame, remorse or grief have eaten at her core, and vacant eyes say that something inside is broken. Her once satin skin is all sallow.

Bats dangle upside-down overhead. Waves out yonder crash against the cliff.

"Behind me, chile," says Auntie Azikiwe in her soft honey voice. "Umozi?"

The ghost of Aunt Umozi stays head bent.

"We can talk about calamity," says Auntie Azikiwe. "Or redemption."

Umozi shudders, then looks up in a squint at Goddess Mother's dazzle as she walks quietly, deeper into the inner cave, closely followed by Phoena and Bibi, the sea ghost.

"We have a mission," says the goddess kindly to Umozi. "So I want you to make an effort."

Umozi quietly weeps.

"It is not a request," the goddess says sternly. "You have done enough damage."

Umozi, still crying, her face buried in dishevelled braids, now sways in wretchedness.

"Let me,' says Auntie Azikiwe. She beckons Phoena, who unfolds her wings and holds out the baby. He is fully dry and happy.

"Ga ga ga ga."

Umozi stills at Imani's gurgle. Auntie Azikiwe takes Imani, steps forward and lays him on Umozi's lap.

Umozi starts to tremble.

*Namulee, Namulee…* the sea ghost is uncertain. Azikiwe holds up a hand.

The phoenix's song is scatter and want, fragments and plea. Stars sparkle in her ruby eyes and plumage that has stolen the red-gold moon's face. Her lyrics are wild and slipping, painting watercolours of marigolds and poppies, questing for twilight worlds that lend love by dawn. Resurrection is silence, a gyration of clemency that demands nothing back.

"Ga ga ga ga." Fat arms reach for one of Umozi's braids. She stiffens, as if afraid of herself, her capacity to harm. Slowly, gently, her hand finally touches his head and strokes his tight black curls. His ebony gaze that glints silver holds her own, then he smiles, all gap-toothed.

Umozi's face softens. She looks in wonderment, first at Azikiwe, then at the baby. A lone tear falls down her cheek. She puts a careful hand under the baby's head and brings him close to her chest. As she gently rocks him, a golden-brown colour returns to her skin. She begins to glow, as if rebirthed. Imani rests his cheek on her shoulder and sucks two middle fingers.

His eyes droop and he falls asleep.

Namu lets out a big cry and runs out of the cave.

#

They stand on a beach as the sky blackens. Namulongo's spelling has kept furious rain from them in a dry ring. The world trembles and roars around their magic circle.

Together, unbidden, they hold hands—Namu will not touch Umozi's, so Auntie Azi is between them. They dance in a chant around baby Imani in the middle on the ground. He is sucking his fingers, ankles together above ground.

Namu gazes inwards and sways in a chant.

*Maga kasi*

*Osi osi.*

Azikiwe glares and hisses her chant.

*Rozi tasi*

*Navi dato.*

Umozi flows in silence and grace, glowing brighter, together with Goddess Mother.

"Ga ga ga ga," the baby gurgles. The silver in his eyes is a blaze that pierces the skies. Imani levitates, the goddess too. It doesn't matter whose power yields it, but Namu finds herself floating on air too, together with Auntie Azikiwe and Aunt Umozi.

Together they are. A quadity of magi, a phoenix, a sea ghost and a goddess mother. Now they're a ball of light soaring towards the skies. A crackle of lightning, then a big and terrible sound ushers the arrival of Tamoi, Posé and Daga.

*Maga kasi*
*Osi osi!*

~

*Rozi tasi*
*Navi dato!*

~

"Ga ga ga ga," the baby gurbles.

The ball of light swirls, swirls across the firmament, then hurtles at speed towards Posé, Tamoi and Daga—who have no magic but bear might. Posé's clever mind fails to predict the mind of a collective. Daga's lab has formed mammoth cyclops that thunderbolt from pins and marbles, but they too are no match for a multiplicity that is a ball of light.

Tamoi routs a giant forked tree, roots and all, and hurls with all his might. The giant globule of light swallows the tree, then spits it larger, sharper and faster.

The tree spears into Tamoi, who manages to put his shattered self together, but is shaken. Finally, all three, Posé, Tamoi and Daga are sprawled on their backs, the ball of light crushing them to dust. Still they reform to their selves, and they posture in attack stance, yet dare not approach. Inside the light, Namu feels herself spin.

"Stop!" cries Posé.

"Please!" Tamoi's bellow.

"We surrender!" Daga has his hands in the air.

"Maé-maé," gurgles Imani, and the ball of light softly lands and opens: a petal.

The rain at once stops and a bright sun whitens the sky.

Goddess Mother, Aunt Umozi, Auntie Azikiwe, Phoena, Namu, Bibi and Imani emerge from the globule. Imani creeps on hands and knees to Tamoi. He stands himself up Tamoi's knees. Unafraid of the horn where Tamoi's nose should be, the baby raises his hands to be picked up.

Tamoi complies, more in trepidation than in fondness.

Imani puts his fat palms on the horn and breaks it off, just like that.

Tamoi screams, lets go the baby, who swoons unharmed into the sea ghost's fog. All eyes are on Tamoi, quietened, hands on his face. He traces the path of the lost horn and the smoothness of his beauty—reborn.

## Hugging the Marula Tree

The goddess studied the toddler. Imani was a quick study of nature and gave himself to flowers, worms, beetles and trees. He put everything into his mouth, from grass, twigs, soil to mopane worms.

"Maé-maé," he spoke his two new words, the only ones he murmured to denote anything that could be hunger, thirst, ouchy, look-look!

There was beauty in possibility, poetry in belief, the cantata of a new tomorrow. Now the bub pushed himself up from the grass, toddled a few steps and fell on his bum. He clapped his hands in glee and let Goddess Mother take his hand to better his wobble as she guided him to where he pointed with a finger.

"Maé-maé." He hugged the ankle of a marula tree, and willed with his gaze at the unripe fruit, grabbed two that fell into his fat hands and banged them together. "Maé-maé," he gurgled.

His was a prophecy unmasked in a paradise that could never be too much.

"Is it over?" asked Azikiwe. Her meaning was clear: Goddess Mother's temporal banishment of Posé, Tamoi and

Daga from Savanna.

"Until when?" Tamoi had cried.

"Until you properly contemplate your actions that pushed your sister to take such drastic measures," goddess mother had said.

"But Goddess Mother—" Daga tried.

"Sometimes a hen breaks its own egg to make room in her nest for the rest of the eggs to blossom," she'd said with finality.

The goddess thought for a moment. She glanced at Namulongo cavorting in the crystal lake with the white rhino, the sabre-toothed tiger and the slow and awkward dodo. The homing spell, Tila, whistling, blowing bubbles—at home in this world. When Namu wasn't frolicking with the pets, the girl was a controlled rage, a smouldering just beneath the surface. She left space, any space, when Umozi neared it.

Still, they hadn't spoken.

"It's never over," Goddess Mother said. "It. Never. Is."

Because a tree always, always remembers.

*Namulee, Namulee…* the sea ghost drinks their dread.

Discover Luna Novella in our store:

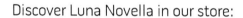

https://www.lunapresspublishing.com/shop

Printed in the USA
CPSIA information can be obtained
at www.ICGtesting.com
JSHW020828200124
55354JS00005B/175